EDGAR RICE BURROUGHS'
Tarzan®
IN COLOR

HOGARTH–

Volume 11
(1941-1942)

FLYING
BUTTRESS
classics
library

**A special edition signed by Burne Hogarth
limited and numbered to 320 is available of this book.
$60 each or $180 for a subscription to 4 volumes.**

Special thanks to the following collectors
who helped us find the best reproduction:
Gale Paulson

Tarzan weekly pages numbers 549 through 600 are
© 1941, 1942 EDGAR RICE BURROUGHS, INC., All Rights Reserved.
© NBM 1995

LC #93-84318
ISBN 1-56163-121-3
Production: Ying Gu
Printed in Hong Kong

Trademark TARZAN owned by
EDGAR RICE BURROUGHS, INC.,
and used by permission.

Flying Buttress Classics Library
is an imprint of:

NANTIER · BEALL · MINOUSTCHINE

Publishing inc.

new york

Tarzan

THE DEATH OF A HUNDRED CUTS:

The Newspaper Guillotining of the Hogarth Sunday Page in World War II

by Bill Blackbeard

S urrounded by the disembowelled newsprint of a dozen mid-1943 Sunday comic sections from a dozen different cities and holding the brutally truncated *Tarzan* episode he had found in each one - picked up one mid-week afternoon at an out-of-town-newspaper store near his studio - Burne Hogarth might well have entertained a brooding fantasy along the line of the sad fable of hopeless heroics that follows...

There were a multitude of heroes on all fronts in the second World War: heroes on the battlefields, in the production lines, in the laboratories, everywhere.

Everywhere, that is, except in a feature editor's chair in any American Sunday newspaper office.

A hero *might* have sat in such a chair at some point between 1942 and the end of the war, *might* have seen what had to be done at one newspaper at least to kindle similar heroisms elsewhere, to start the ball rolling, to save a large part of the dignity of a unique American art form in at least one place, at least for a while.

Might have, but didn't.

Suppose, though, that our absent hero had existed. Suppose that his Sunday comic section, prior to 1943, consisted of 16 full-size color pages, about half of which carried such major full-page comics as *Li'l Abner, Little Orphan Annie, Dick Tracy, Flash Gordon* (with its *Jungle Jim* topper), *Alley Oop, Captain Easy*, and - of course - *Tarzan*. In the remaining half of the color pages were a few standard sets of half-page combos, such as *Mickey Mouse/Donald Duck, Terry and the Pirates/Smilin' Jack, Room and Board/The Squirrel Cage*, and *The Captain and the Kids/Hawkshaw the Detective*, plus a few more isolated half-pages accompanied by the three or four half-page ads that paid for the section. A section, actually, not notably out of line with many such sections of the time.

Comes 1943, a newsprint cost-squeeze, a general down-sizing of newspapers in terms of pages, and our make-believe hero is confronted with the need to reorganize his color comic section into a maximum ten pages (and that only when there are at least four half-page ads to cover its cost; otherwise eight pages will have to do). In effect, our heroic feature editor has had his section chopped in half. Now heavy pressure is on this

Tarzan

by Edgar Rice Burroughs

BETWEEN TWO FOES

TARZAN TRIED TO SHAPE A BOW-- IN VAIN. THE MOIST WOOD LACKED SPRINGINESS.

SO HE HAD NOTHING BUT HIS KNIFE AS A WEAPON AGAINST HIS FOE'S LONG-RANGE RIFLE. SO HE SET OUT AGAIN---- ---

TO SEARCH FOR THE DANGEROUS HERMIT--TO KILL FIRST OR BE KILLED!

BUT SLY NAHRO KEPT TO HIS HIDING PLACE, HOPING TO UNNERVE TARZAN BY THE MYSTERY OF HIS DISAPPEARANCE.

AT MIDDAY THE APE-MAN WAS EXPLORING A SECTION OF SWAMPLAND, WEIRD AND DISMAL.

AS HE PENETRATED THE SWAMP ALONG A PENINSULA OF DRY LAND, HE TURNED SUDDENLY AS WAS HIS EVER CAUTIOUS HABIT.

THERE, IN THE DISTANCE HE SAW THE HUNTER, WHO HAD MYSTERIOUSLY REAPPEARED TO STALK HIM.

AS TARZAN HURRIED TO LOSE HIMSELF IN THE SWAMP, HE SAW A HUGE RHINOCEROS.

THE EYES OF THE RHINO WERE WEAK, BUT THE WIND BORE TO ITS KEEN NOSTRILS THE HATED SCENT OF THE INTRUDER.

THE FEROCIOUS BEAST PAWED THE EARTH, SNORTING WITH FURY.

TARZAN MIGHT HAVE ESCAPED, BUT NOW HE CONCEIVED A PLAN THAT REQUIRED HIM TO KILL THE MIGHTY MONSTER. BOLDLY HE STRODE FORWARD. THEN THE RHINO CHARGED! ﹦NEXT WEEK﹦ PIT OF DEATH!

guy, from the advertising department, the strip syndicates, and a fair number of readers, to keep *all* of the extant strips in the reduced section by simply cutting the full-page strips to half-pages, retaining a few previous half-pages as such, and slashing the remaining half-pages into third-pagers. The newspaper advertising department is fearful of any dip in circulation that might result from an offended group of readers cancelling subscriptions because of a favorite strip being dropped or because of a perceived loss of variety resulting from several strips being tossed out to accomodate the six to eight page cut. The syndicates are, of course, eager to maintain the same level of revenue as before from the continuing publication of the same number of strips in reduced sizes in our hero's paper. And a good number of vocal readers will scream at the omission of any strip or strips. (They won't scream, however, at the downgrading in strip size itself, since *that* can be readily attributed to wartime shortages of paper and ink.)

No dilemma for all of the other feature editors in the country. Strips are an annoying public-relations commodity most of them detest anyway, and a good squeezing is just what they deserve. But our hero, being *our* hero, is distressed. He sees and appreciates the visual and narrative impact of strips appearing in the formats established by artists and syndicates over past decades when display size was not affected by paper limitations, and is appalled by the loss of much of this impact in the new crippling sizes being urged on him from all quarter. (Even the layout mats and proofs being sent him by the syndicates are a shock: full-page mats have been abandoned totally, and he is being provided only half-page and third-page mats as his jolly Hobson's choice in laying out his now truncated section.)

Defying all pressures, our hero decides to opt for quality over quantity, and sees a way to get away with it. He has noted that such long-established color comic sections as those of the *New York Sunday News* and the *New York Sunday Mirror* are continuing to publish their major strips in the reduced full-page size known as the tabloid-page format. Fine. He informs the syndicates that he is thinking of turning his paper's comic section to a tabloid format, and requests tabloid full-page strip layouts from them. They are duly sent. And our hero, who defies the prevailing feature editor mode by being smart as well as heroic, proceeds to have his own newspaper's layout department *enlarge* the tabloid proofs to full-page normality, make new mats, and go to press with his first ten-page comic section.

The result is terrific to his delighted eyes. *Tarzan, Li'l Abner, Annie, Tracy, Oop, Easy,* and others gone to half-pages or tabloids everywhere else in the country continue in their established full-page glory in *his* comic section. A few first-rate half-pages continue in their full size. The others, sadly but necessarily, are dropped, to preserve the dignity of the best that remain. A dynamic wrap. The major newsmagazines (having no commercial stake in any of this, and having been apprised in advance of our smart hero's plans, *by* our hero), ladle out deserved praises for this remarkable strike at maintaining the creative integrity of the best strips. Gilbert Seldes sings his praises further in *Esquire*. "Quality Picked Over Quantity" headlines a startled report in *Editor and Publisher*. But the rest is silence. The nation's other newspapers, of course, print no coverage. Their readers are not to know that such things are even conceivable, let alone possible. The

TARZAN

BETWEEN TWO FOES   by Edgar Rice Burroughs

BUT SLY NAHRO KEPT TO HIS HIDING PLACE, HOPING TO UNNERVE TARZAN BY THE MYSTERY OF HIS DISAPPEARANCE.

"TO SEARCH FOR THE DANGEROUS HERMIT—TO KILL FIRST OR BE KILLED!

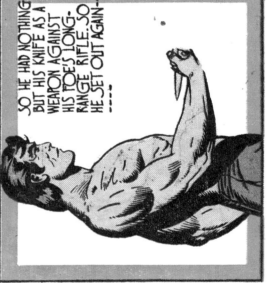

SO HE HAD NOTHING BUT HIS KNIFE AS A WEAPON AGAINST HIS FOE'S LONG-RANGE RIFLE. SO HE SET OUT AGAIN---

TARZAN TRIED TO SHAPE A BOW—IN VAIN. THE MOIST WOOD LACKED SPRINGINESS.

AS TARZAN HURRIED TO LOSE HIMSELF IN THE SWAMP, HE SAW A HUGE RHINOCEROS.

THERE, IN THE DISTANCE HE SAW THE HUNTER, WHO HAD MYSTERIOUSLY REAPPEARED TO STALK HIM.

AT MIDDAY THE APE-MAN WAS EXPLORING A SECTION OF SWAMPLAND, WEIRD AND DISMAL.

AS HE PENETRATED THE SWAMP ALONG A PENINSULA OF DRY LAND HE TURNED SUDDENLY AS WAS HIS EVER CAUTIOUS HABIT.

—HOGARTH—

TARZAN MIGHT HAVE ESCAPED, BUT NOW HE CONCEIVED A PLAN THAT REQUIRED HIM TO KILL THE MIGHTY MONSTER. BOLDLY HE STRODE FORWARD. THEN THE RHINO CHARGED—NEXT WEEK: PIT OF DEATH!

THE FEROCIOUS BEAST PAWED THE EARTH, SNORTING WITH FURY.

THE EYES OF THE RHINO WERE WEAK, BUT THE WIND BORE TO ITS KEEN NOSTRILS THE HATED SCENT OF THE INTRUDER.

strips they are given each Sunday are the only strips there are, of course. (And sadly, that is just what most newspaper readers believed then, just as they do in 1995.) And what of our imagined hero's paper?

It fires him.

And within a short time, his comic section - his no more - reverts to the half-page national *diktat* that prevails everywhere.

So much for being a hero. But just such ultimately suicidal behavior is what it *would* have taken in 1943, when America's national newspaper razor sliced virtually all of its Sunday comics down to half size or less in the name of wartime necessity, to stand up even briefly against what was being undertaken, justifiably to most in the name of continuing syndicate and artist income, and to assure the readers' Pavlovian comfort in seeing all of their favorites continuing in print, regardless of how they looked in this deliberate demeaning of their intrinsic creative potential.

Needless to say, once the war was over, the emergency changes in strip format remained permanently in place, to become even worse over the next few decades. The syndicates were happy to be able to place more small-format features in newspapers, at the same income per feature, than they were able to sell in the pre-war years. The newpapers were pleased, able to present more strips to their readers in less newprint space than before the war, while the insufferably submoronic populace, relishing a *Nancy* or an *Eek and Meek* for accelerated reading where they had once had to push hardily forward through the marvellously weighty wordage of *The Bungle Family* or *Thimble Theatre*, thought all of the stacked rows of simply drawn vignettes with their Joe Miller, he-said, she-said gags were simply marvellous. That an art had been permanently crippled seemed to bother no one.

No one, that is, except those artists whose creative hopes and ambitions went considerably beyond mere gratefulness at the retention of an income in a wartime and post-war field of deliberately reduced newsprint space. (Of course the hack space-fillers of syndicate package-sale deals who drew such awesome drek as *Dotty Dripple*, *Ozark Ike*, *Don Winslow of the Navy*, *Don Dixon*, and Gus Edson's *Gumps*, were tickled blushing pink at the space reduction rescue of work such as theirs, since a qualitative size-retention policy in national comic sections of fewer pages would have seen a long-deserved trip to oblivion for all of them.) But the gifted artists of memorable comic or dramatic graphic power, such as Hogarth, had to take the structural slashing of their printed work like a bayonet twist in the creative gut. They would recover and continue, but the crippling pain would stay in the reproduction of their work from then on.

What happened can be seen in the comic pages printed in 1943 and later. Fine lines that heightened and sustained a given graphic mood and sense of narrative reality in pages such as *Tarzan* were crudely thickened or even blurred together in much of the half-page printing, forcing the artists to simplify such vital penwork thereafter. Crucial scenic or action details could be skewed into distorted obscurity in strip halves by the same mild off-registration of color that would pass almost unnoticed in the full-page format, again leaving the artist with no choice but to de-vitalize his work by enlarging figures and

graphic story elements in all panels to fend off the effect of frequent fast-press mis-registry of color. Full exposition in dialogue and the sort of narrative text carried in Tarzan had to dumbed and simplified down to remain readable in the half-page layout. These changes, painful and sharply evident to the artists and those readers sensitively concerned about such elements, went unnoticed by the general public and by most of the news and critical media (the cultural status of comics being what they were at the time), thus - of course - delighting syndicate executives who realized they would face no serious public relations problems in retaining the conveniently reduced strip sizes after the war.

The foregoing account of the 1943 Sunday (and daily) strip format disaster and its aftermath has been somewhat simplified in itself here for dramatic emphasis. Not all strips were reduced in size by all syndicates simultaneously; the reductions were actually phased in over the course of a year or so. Some papers did indeed try to hold on to full-page formats for strips that were particular favorites of readers (and even of abnormally bright feature editors): *Li'l Abner* appeared in full-page format in a number of papers well into 1944, until Capp's enforced dumbing-down of panel graphics for most papers that had gone to halves became embarrassing in the large size, and led to its being dropped even by the hold-outs. Again, a handful of major cartoonists fought format simplication for years, holding to the quality of detail and dialogue they had pursued in the past: Caniff, Crane, Hamlin, and - needless to add - Hogarth himself were among these. (Harold Foster, favored of the syndicate god named William Randolph Hearst, was permitted to continue his *Prince Valiant* as a full page in all Hearst newspapers through the war and after.) In the post-war era, too, a few hopeful syndicates tried strips as *Lance, Johnny Reb, Dick's Adventures in Dreamland*, etc., but without obtaining a secure, long-term foothold.

And Hogarth did, in fact, find himself a couple of genuine feature-editor heroes. On the *Boston Globe* and the *Reno Gazette* (and for a time at least in a few small-town papers), editors forthrightly continued to run *Tarzan* from 1943 on into the 1950s as a full-page strip, while the doughty *Oakland Tribune* stuck with the strip in full format until very late in the war years, long after Hogarth's own syndicate had given the strip over to only half-page, tabloid, and third-page release formats.

Most of the pages being used in the present NBM reprint series have been from the *Oakland Tribune* (and from the *Los Angeles Times*, until the *Times* went the way of the national press in general and dropped the Hogarth work to half-page in 1943); in the future, the post-war fulls from the *Reno Gazette* will be utilized for the most part. However, even these sources fell back occasionally in the depth of the war years to half-pages, while the bound files which yielded up the pages we have on hand would sometimes turn out to have Sunday sections omitted, forcing us to turn to other sources for reprint material. We would, consequently, greatly appreciate anyone among our readers, or known to them, who might have a file of Tarzan full-pages from 1943 through 1947 (including the infamous Rubimor pages) to contact the NBM publishing office at 185 Madison Avenue, Suite 1504, New York, NY 10016 and let us know what they have on hand. There is remuneration and clippings are treated with great care.

RIDDLED BY THE BULLETS HE HAD INVITED FROM HIS CAPTORS, STOUT KING KORNAK TURNED TO HIS PEOPLE.

"YOU CAME TO SURRENDER, TO SAVE ME. NOW THERE IS NO NEED TO SACRIFICE YOUR FREEDOM----- FAREWELL, IBEKS---FIGHT ON!"

Copr. 1941, Edgar Rice Burroughs, Inc—Tm. Reg. U.S Pat. Off. Distr. by United Feature Syndicate, Inc

LIKE A FELLED OAK, THE VALIANT MONARCH CRASHED TO EARTH.

THE IBEKS STOOD IN SILENT TRIBUTE TO THEIR KING, WHO HAD GIVEN HIS LIFE TO CANCEL THEIR PLEDGE OF SURRENDER.

THEN THEY WERE SEIZED WITH VENGEFUL FURY. "TO ARMS!" THEY SHOUTED. "STORM THE FORT! DEATH TO THE TYRANT!"

AS THEY TOOK UP THEIR ARMS, TARZAN TRIED TO DISSUADE THEM FROM A SUICIDAL DAYLIGHT RAID.

HE EXPLAINED THE POWER OF THE FORT'S MACHINE GUN. THE IBEKS DOUBTED THAT SUCH A WEAPON EXISTED.

HOWEVER, LIKE MANY MEN-AT-ARMS, THEY HAD BLIND FAITH IN THEIR ACCUSTOMED INSTRUMENTS OF WAR.

"IF TARZAN IS A COWARD, LET HIM GO HIS OWN WAY," ONE GROWLED; "WE WILL FIGHT!"

KAMUR TRUSTED TARZAN'S WARNING. HE TRIED TO HALT HIS FRENZIED MEN. WHEN HE FAILED, HE JOINED THEM, CRYING:

"NEVER SHALL IT BE SAID THAT KAMUR WAS NOT IN THE VANGUARD OF HIS FIGHTERS!"

HOGARTH

THEN AS HE SPRINTED AHEAD, HE GASPED WITH ASTONISHMENT. THERE WAS TARZAN-- RUNNING AWAY!

NEXT WEEK: PERILOUS GOAL

Tarzan
by Edgar Rice Burroughs

PERILOUS GOAL

DESPITE TARZAN'S WARNING, THE IBEK WARRIORS WITH THEIR PRIMITIVE WEAPONS CHARGED THE WELL-ARMED FORT.

AND KAMUR, WHO CONSIDERED TARZAN THE BRAVEST OF THE BRAVE, WAS ASTONISHED TO SEE HIM RUNNING AWAY.

MEANWHILE, IN THE FORT, DAGGA RAMBA ORDERED HIS FULL FORCE TO THE SOUTH WALL, FACING THE FOE.

HE CALLED TO THE MACHINE GUN CREW ATOP THE WALL: "WHEN I GIVE THE WORD, MOW THEM DOWN!"

THEN THE DARK EMPEROR ASSURED HIS OWN SAFETY BY ENTERING AN ARMORED TURRET.

NOW, WHILE THE EYES OF THE ASKARIS WERE FIXED ON THE IBEKS, TARZAN WAS CIRCLING THE FORT.

WITH THE TAN OF HIS BODY AS A NATURAL CAMOUFLAGE, HE GAINED THE NORTH WALL UNDETECTED.

Copr. 1941.

HE CREPT WARILY THROUGH THE FORT, TO THE BACKS OF THE ASKARIS.

HIS PURPOSE WAS TO DESTROY THE DEADLY MACHINE GUN AND SAVE THE IBEKS FROM DESTRUCTION.

WHEN, SUDDENLY, AN ASKARI HAPPENED TO TURN AROUND!

NEXT WEEK: FATEFUL ARROW

HOGARTH
550
9-21-41

TARZAN DODGED THROUGH AN OPEN DOORWAY—INTO A NEW CRISIS!

Tarzan

by Edgar Rice Burroughs

FATEFUL ARROW

AS THE ASKARI TURNED, TARZAN DODGED INTO A DOORWAY--AND FOUND HIMSELF IN TA'AMA'S ROOM.

"TARZAN!" SHE EXCLAIMED; "I KNEW YOU LOVED ME. YOU'VE COME TO TAKE ME AWAY."

TARZAN ANSWERED GRIMLY: "YOU MUST STAY. THE LIVES OF MANY IBEKS DEPEND ON ME NOW. YOU ARE IN NO DANGER."

THE FIERY DESERT MAID WAS ANGERED. "TAKE ME AWAY AT ONCE, OR I'LL SCREAM AND BRING THE SOLDIERS!"

TARZAN FIXED HER WITH A GAZE OF CONFIDENT AUTHORITY. "NO, YOU WILL NOT BETRAY ME!"

THE APE-MAN CREPT TO THE DOOR. THE COAST WAS CLEAR. WARILY HE RESUMED HIS HAZARDOUS COURSE.

NOW DAGGA RAMBA GAVE THE ORDER TO FIRE ON THE IBEK HORDE. RIFLES CRACKED. THE MACHINE GUN CHATTERED.

TARZAN THREW CAUTION ASIDE. HE MUST ACT BOLDLY TO SAVE THE IBEKS FROM THE MACHINE GUN'S HAVOC.

HIS LASSO SAILED THROUGH THE AIR AND ENCIRCLED THE GUN BARREL. HE JERKED VIOLENTLY.

THE WEAPON CRASHED TO EARTH. IT WAS WRECKED. IN THE CONFUSION, THE APE-MAN RACED TO THE WALL TO ESCAPE.

HE SPRANG SIDEWISE, TO KEEP HIS FOES IN VIEW. AS ONE HAND CLUTCHED THE TOP OF THE WALL-----

--A STRAY IBEK ARROW STRUCK IT. TARZAN'S GRIP WAS BROKEN. HE FELL BACK TO THE GROUND!

HOGARTH 9-28-41 SS1

NEXT WEEK: QUICK AND DESPERATE

Tarzan

by Edgar Rice Burroughs

QUICK AND DESPERATE

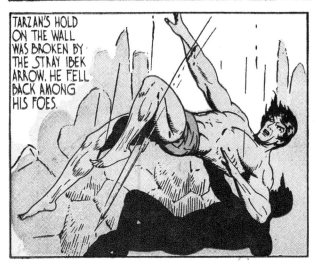

TARZAN'S HOLD ON THE WALL WAS BROKEN BY THE STRAY IBEK ARROW. HE FELL BACK AMONG HIS FOES.

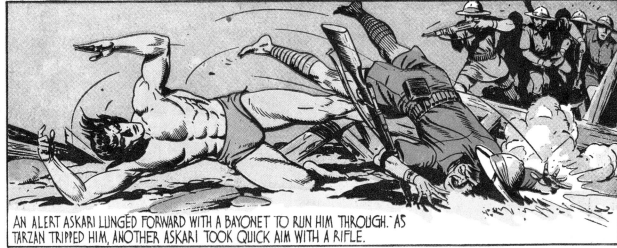

AN ALERT ASKARI LUNGED FORWARD WITH A BAYONET TO RUN HIM THROUGH. AS TARZAN TRIPPED HIM, ANOTHER ASKARI TOOK QUICK AIM WITH A RIFLE.

EMERGING FROM HIS TURRET, DAGGA RAMBA CRIED OUT: "HOLD YOUR FIRE!"

"TARZAN'S EXECUTION IS A PLEASURE I CLAIM FOR MYSELF." THEN TARZAN MOVED LIKE LIGHTNING.

BEFORE THE RIFLEMEN COULD INTERFERE, HE HAD PLANTED HIS KNIFE AT DAGGA RAMBA'S CHEST.

Copr. 1941

"IF ANYONE MAKES A MOVE AGAINST ME," HE SAID GRIMLY: "I'LL PLUNGE THIS THROUGH YOUR HEART."

"DON'T-DON'T!" THE DESPOT QUAVERED, "I'LL GIVE YOU SAFE CONDUCT FROM THE FORT."

TARZAN CONSIDERED. IT WOULD BE A VICTORY INDEED TO ESCAPE THIS HORNET'S NEST OF ENEMIES.

"I'LL AGREE," HE REPLIED, "IF YOU'LL FREE PRINCESS TA'AMA TO GO WITH ME." DAGGA RAMBA CONSENTED EAGERLY.

SHIEK NUMALI OVERHEARD. TA'AMA WAS VITAL TO HIS OWN DARK PLANS. HE'D NOT LET TARZAN TAKE HER AWAY. HE BECKONED TO HIS HENCHMAN—

HOGARTH—

---AND WHISPERED MYSTERIOUSLY. THE FELLOW HURRIED AWAY TO DO HIS BIDDING.

NEXT WEEK: TREACHERY

Tarzan

by Edgar Rice Burroughs

TREACHERY

TARZAN HELD THE KNIFE AT DAGGA RAMBA'S BREAST, READY TO THRUST IF ANYONE THREATENED HIM.

"LET NO ONE MAKE A MOVE AGAINST TARZAN," THE DARK EMPEROR QUAVERED.

"NOW, HAVE TA'AMA BROUGHT TO ME," THE APE-MAN COMMANDED, "AND I SHALL GO." THEN NUMALI INTERVENED.

"SHE'S BEEN TAKEN SUDDENLY ILL. SHE CANNOT TRAVEL. BESIDES, DAGGA RAMBA HAS GUARANTEED HER SAFETY."

"I DO NOT TRUST YOU," THE JUNGLE LORD GROWLED; "I'LL SEE FOR MY-SELF!"

WALKING BACKWARD SO HE COULD KEEP HIS EYES ON THE ASKARIS, HE TOOK HIS HOSTAGE WITH HIM.

MEANWHILE, NUMALI'S HENCHMAN HAD DONE HIS EVIL WORK. SLIPPING UP BEHIND TA'AMA, HE KNOCKED HER SENSELESS.

THEN HE TRANSFERRED HER HASTILY TO HER BED.

WHEN TARZAN CAME IN, THE SCOUNDREL WAS TENDING HER WITH MOCK DEVOTION.

"A TOUCH OF THE SUN, OR SOMETHING," NUMALI SHRUGGED, "IT WOULD BE DANGEROUS TO MOVE HER!"

"VERY WELL," TARZAN AGREED. "BUT IF HARM COMES TO HER, YOU'LL PAY--- NOW, I RETURN TO THE IBEKS."

DAGGA RAMBA SMILED TO HIMSELF. HE SAW A WAY TO DESTROY TARZAN!

NEXT WEEK: **IN DEFENSE OF A FOE**

Tarzan
by Edgar Rice Burroughs
IN DEFENSE OF A FOE

WHEN TARZAN SAID HE WAS READY TO RETURN TO THE IBEKS, DAGGA RAMBA SMILED INWARDLY.

IT WOULD BE SIMPLE TO PUT A BULLET IN TARZAN AS HE CROSSED THE PLAIN.

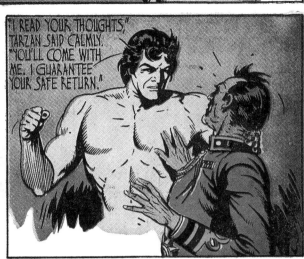

"I READ YOUR THOUGHTS," TARZAN SAID CALMLY. "YOU'LL COME WITH ME, I GUARANTEE YOUR SAFE RETURN."

MEANWHILE, THE IBEKS HAD RETREATED UNDER THE FIRST DEADLY VOLLEY OF GUNFIRE.

NOW THEY REFORMED RANKS AND RENEWED THEIR WILD CHARGE, SO FOOLISH YET SO VALIANT.

THOUGH TARZAN HAD BROKEN THE FORT'S MACHINE GUN, HE KNEW THE IBEKS WOULD SUFFER HEAVILY FROM RIFLE FIRE.

NOW HE DRAPED HIS HOSTAGE ACROSS HIS SHOULDER AS A SHIELD AGAINST A TREACHEROUS SHOT.

THEN HE RUSHED OUT IN A HAIL OF ARROWS. THE ASTONISHED IBEKS DREW BACK AND AWAITED HIM.

"HE'S CAPTURED DAGGA RAMBA!" THEY SHOUTED; "WE'LL KILL THE VIPER!"

"NO! I'VE GUARANTEED HIS SAFETY," TARZAN OBJECTED. "BUT WE'VE MADE NO PROMISE," A WARRIOR ROARED.

AS A BAND OF HOT HEADS RUSHED TO SEIZE THE HOSTAGE, THE JUNGLE LORD GROWLED:

TARZAN HAS GIVEN HIS WORD. HE'LL KEEP IT. THOUGH THIS MAN IS MY FOE, I'LL DEFEND HIM WITH MY LIFE!"

NEXT WEEK: WARNING UNHEEDED

HOGARTH

Tarzan

by Edgar Rice Burroughs

WARNING UNHEEDED

HAVING PLEDGED PAGGA RAMBA'S SAFETY, TARZAN DEFENDED HIM AGAINST THE IBEK HOTHEADS.

KAMUR'S ROYAL AUTHORITY AND A STRONG RIGHTARM HALTED THE MELEE. THEN TARZAN TURNED TO HIS HOSTAGE.

"YOU ARE FREE TO GO, BUT THIS IS NO TRUCE. WE ARE ENEMIES, PAGGA RAMBA-- TO THE DEATH!"

NOW THE WARRIORS TOOK UP THEIR DEAD AND WOUNDED AND MARCHED SOLEMNLY BACK TO THEIR MOUNTAINS.

IN THE DAYS THAT FOLLOWED, THE DARK EMPEROR DISPATCHED RAIDERS TO DESTROY THE IBEKS. THE DEFENDERS WERE BRAVE AND SKILFUL, BUT PRIMITIVE WEAPONS WERE NOT A MATCH FOR RIFLES.

SLOWLY THE RANKS OF THE IBEKS DWINDLED. "SOON WE SHALL BE NO MORE," KAMUR LAMENTED.

"PAGGA RAMBA WILL MENACE THE SOUFARANS, TOO," TARZAN SAID; "I'LL GO AND OFFER THEM AN ALLIANCE!"

KAMUR PROTESTED. "THEIRS IS AN ISOLATED, FORBIDDEN LAND. STRANGERS ARE PUT TO DEATH!"

THEN HE SMILED. "FORTUNATELY YOU CAN'T GO TO SOUFARA. YOU HAVE NO CAMEL TO CROSS THE GREAT DESERT."

"I SHALL GET ONE FROM THE BEDOUINS YONDER," TARZAN SAID CONFIDENTLY. KAMUR TRIED TO RESTRAIN HIM.

HOGARTH—

NEXT WEEK: DESERT MARKSMAN!

"...THE BEDOUINS ARE DANGEROUS. YOU MUST NOT VENTURE AMONG THEM." "I'LL GO," TARZAN ANSWERED CALMLY.

Tarzan

by Edgar Rice Burroughs

DESERT MARKSMEN

KAMUR WARNED TARZAN NOT TO VENTURE AMONG THE FIERCE BEDOUINS.

"IF YOU MUST, I'LL GO WITH YOU," HE SAID. "I'LL TAKE THE RISK ALONE," TARZAN ANSWERED. THEN HE BEGAN THE DESCENT INTO THE DESERT.

AS HE NEARED THE CAMP, ARMED BEDOUINS GATHERED BEFORE THE TENTS. "SALAAM ALEIKUM," TARZAN GREETED.

THE OLD SHEIK CAME FORWARD AND HANDED TARZAN A FEATHER. "WHAT'S THIS?" THE JUNGLE LORD INQUIRED.

"PEACE TO YOU," THE BEDOUINS REPLIED, BUT THEY DID NOT RELAX THEIR VIGILANCE.

"IF YOU HOLD IT AT ARM'S LENGTH, YOU'LL DISCOVER ITS PURPOSE."

ALWAYS WILLING TO CONFORM TO THE CUSTOMS OF STRANGE TRIBES, TARZAN DID AS HE WAS ASKED.

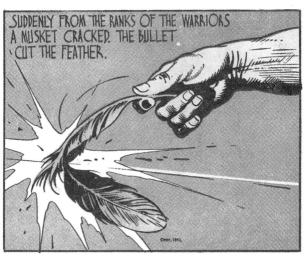

SUDDENLY FROM THE RANKS OF THE WARRIORS A MUSKET CRACKED. THE BULLET CUT THE FEATHER.

THE SHEIK SMILED. "IT IS OUR CUSTOM TO SHOW OUR MARKSMANSHIP AS A WARNING TO THOSE WHO WOULD DO US EVIL."

"I NEED A CAMEL," TARZAN SAID ABRUPTLY, "I'M BOUND FOR SOUFARA TO FIND ALLIES AGAINST DAGGA RAMBA!"

"DAGGA RAMBA IS DANGEROUS," THE SHIEK GRUNTED; "WE'LL NOT OFFEND HIM BY AIDING HIS FOES. WE'LL GIVE YOU NO CAMEL!"

"I INTEND TO HAVE ONE," THE APE-MAN SAID. THE SHEIK SCOWLED. "YOU'D DO WELL TO REMEMBER THE FEATHER!"

HOGARTH—
NEXT WEEK: TRIGGER FINGERS

Tarzan
by Edgar Rice Burroughs

TRIGGER FINGERS

THE BEDOUINS REFUSED TO LEND TARZAN A CAMEL TO CROSS THE DESERT IN QUEST OF ALLIES AGAINST DAGGA RAMBA. "SOME DAY DAGGA RAMBA WILL TURN ON YOU," HE ARGUED. THE SHORT-SIGHTED BEDOUINS WERE NOT PERSUADED.

"THEN AGAINST YOUR WISH, I'LL BORROW A CAMEL", THE APE MAN SAID. THEY LAUGHED AT HIS AUDACITY.

"IF YOU CAN MAKE AWAY WITH A CAMEL—AND YOUR LIFE, TOO—YOU'RE WELCOME TO BOTH," THE SHIEK CHUCKLED.

"I THANK YOU IN ADVANCE," TARZAN SMILED, "FOR I'LL SOON BE VERY BUSY ACCEPTING YOUR GIFT!"

WITH LIGHTNING SPEED HE DARTED BEHIND A TENT. THE STARTLED BEDOUINS FOLLOWED AS HE DODGED IN AND OUT.

THEY DARED NOT FIRE AT THE FUGITIVE FOR FEAR OF ENDANGERING THEIR WOMEN AND CHILDREN.

AMONG THE TENTS TARZAN FOUND A CAMEL HE HAD SEEN WANDERING FROM THE HERD.

THE OLD SHEIK FORESAW TARZAN'S PLAN. "WE'LL WAIT," HE WHISPERED, "AND WHEN HE RIDES OUT WE'LL SHOOT."

TARZAN YELLED TO THE BEAST. "HI-YAH!" IT STARTED TO RUN. THE APE-MAN LEAPED ABOARD.

A MOMENT LATER THE HEAD OF THE RUNNING CAMEL EMERGED FROM BEHIND A TENT.

NEXT WEEK: DOOMED TO LOSE. THE FINGERS OF THE DESERT MARKSMEN BENT AROUND THE TRIGGERS OF THEIR MUSKETS!

Tarzan

by Edgar Rice Burroughs

DOOMED TO LOSE

EXPECTING TO SEE THE ELUSIVE TARZAN MOUNTED ON THE CAMEL, THE DESERT TRIBESMEN MADE READY TO FIRE.

BUT WHEN THE BEAST EMERGED FROM BEHIND THE TENT, TARZAN WAS MISSING.

THE MUSKETEERS WERE ASTONISHED; "HE'S TRICKED US!" THEY SHOUTED.

THEN THEY CAUGHT A GLIMPSE OF THE APE-MAN HANGING TO THE CAMEL ON THE FAR SIDE OF THE HUMP.

"WE CAN'T GET HIM WITHOUT SHOOTING MEHARA, THE CAMEL," THEY CRIED IN DISMAY.

"MEHARA IS OLD AND SLOW," THE SHEIK REMINDED; "AND ON THE OTHER CAMELS WE'LL SOON OVERTAKE HER."

THE DESERT WARRIORS HURRIED TO THE GRAZING HERD AND MOUNTED QUICKLY.

SOON THEY WERE IN HOT PURSUIT OF THEIR QUARRY.

THE RACE HAD HARDLY BEGUN WHEN TARZAN REALIZED HE WAS DOOMED TO LOSE.

UNDER THE APE-MAN'S URGING, OLD MEHARA DID HER BEST, BUT SHE WAS NO MATCH FOR HER SWIFTER AND YOUNGER MATES.

HOGARTH—

TARZAN CROUCHED ON THE NECK OF THE BEAST, SO THAT THE HUMP PROTECTED HIM FROM THE EXPERT MARKSMEN. BUT NOW ONE OF THE PURSUERS SWEPT AROUND AT AN ANGLE TO GET A CLEAR SHOT!

NEXT WEEK: **DEADLY BULLETS**

Tarzan

by Edgar Rice Burroughs

DEADLY BULLETS

THE LONE BEDOUIN WHEELED HIS SWIFT CAMEL TO GET A CLEAR SHOT AT TARZAN. BUT SUDDENLY HE SAW A CLOUD OF DUST RISING FROM THE DESERT. IN ALARM HE SHOUTED TO HIS COMRADES.

TARZAN WAS FORGOTTEN AS THE DUST CLOUD REVEALED A COMPANY OF ASKARIS.

"IT IS DAGGA RAMBA!" THE OLD SHEIK EXCLAIMED. "BUT IS HE NOW A FRIEND OR AN ENEMY?"

DAGGA RAMBA QUICKLY ENDED HIS DOUBTS. DISTANT RIFLES CRACKED, BULLETS SANG PAST THE BEDOUINS.

"CHARGE!" THE FEARLESS NOMADS RODE FORWARD.

THE BEDOUINS' AMMUNITION WAS SCARCE. BUT THEY MADE EVERY BULLET COUNT.

FORESEEING DEFEAT, DAGGA RAMBA TURNED HIS ATTACK UPON THE BEDOUINS' UNGUARDED CAMP.

HE SHOUTED TO THE ONRUSHING WARRIORS: "SURRENDER—OR WE'LL KILL THE WOMEN AND CHILDREN!"

SO, LIFTING MUSKETS ABOVE THEIR HEADS, THE NOMADS RODE SADLY INTO THE CAPTURED CAMP.

THE OLD SHEIK MUTTERED: "TARZAN WAS RIGHT, AFTER ALL. AND NOW HE'LL BRING HELP. ALLAH IS JUST!"

DAGGA RAMBA OVERHEARD HIM! "TARZAN!" HE SAID. "WAS TARZAN HERE? WHERE HAS HE GONE?"

NEXT WEEK: DESERT PURSUIT

HOGARTH—

Tarzan

by Edgar Rice Burroughs

DESERT PURSUIT

"WHERE DID TARZAN GO?" DAGGA RAMBA DEMANDED. "I'LL SAY NOTHING," THE OLD SHIEK ANSWERED.

"SPEAK OR DIE!" THE DARK EMPEROR THREATENED, BUT THE PRISONER STOOD DETERMINED.

"STRIKE IF YOU WILL, BUT I'LL NOT BETRAY TARZAN. HE IS MY FRIEND THOUGH I KNEW IT TOO LATE."

AS THE ANGRY TYRANT PREPARED TO BEHEAD THE OLD MAN, A LITTLE GIRL CRIED OUT:

"SPARE MY FATHER. I'LL SPEAK. TARZAN WENT TO SOUFARA TO BRING THE EMIR'S MEN AGAINST YOU."

THEN SHE ADDED COOLLY: "AND I HOPE THEY KILL YOU, DAGGA RAMBA!"

ELECTRIFIED BY THE NEWS, DAGGA RAMBA GALLOPED AWAY TO THE FORT. THERE HE INSTRUCTED NUMALI:—

"IT IS YOUR TASK TO SEE THAT TARZAN DOES NOT REACH SOUFARA!"

"IF BY CHANCE HE DOES, HE'LL NOT LIVE LONG AFTER," THE SINISTER HENCHMAN REPLIED.

PRESENTLY HE WAS MOUNTED ON A RACING CAMEL, THE SWIFTEST IN ALL THE VAST DESERT. AS HE PASSED THROUGH THE GATEWAY, DAGGA RAMBA CALLED: "DO YOU HAVE PLENTY OF AMMUNITION?"

"PLENTY," NUMALI SAID; "BUT I'LL NEED JUST ONE BULLET. THE FOOLISH TARZAN CARRIES ONLY A KNIFE!"

HOGARTH—

NEXT WEEK: A BULLET STRIKES

Tarzan

A BULLET STRIKES

by EDGAR RICE BURROUGHS

ON HIS SWIFT RACING CAMEL, NUMALI SET OUT ACROSS THE DESERT WASTES TO INTERCEPT THE APE-MAN.

MEANWHILE TARZAN DETOURED TO PICK UP PROVISIONS FROM THE IBEKS, THEN RESUMED HIS JOURNEY TO SOLIFARA.

MEHARA, HIS CAMEL, WAS OLD AND SLOW, BUT THE JUNGLE LORD'S KINDLY COAXING INSPIRED HER TO DO HER BEST.

LATE NEXT DAY, OLD MEHARA BEGAN TO TREMBLE. SHE SNIFFED THE AIR, AND BLEATED UNHAPPILY.

SOON TARZAN SAW THE CAUSE—A GREAT CLOUD OF SAND SWEEPING OVER THE HORIZON—THE DREAD KHAMSIN!

AS WAS HIS CUSTOM AT INTERVALS, THE APE-MAN LOOKED BEHIND. THERE WAS NUMALI, IN SWIFT PURSUIT!

NUMALI FIRED, BUT TARZAN WAS TOO DISTANT FOR ACCURATE AIM. THE BULLET WHISTLED PAST THE APE-MAN.

OLD MEHARA BALKED IN THE FACE OF THE SANDSTORM. SHE WANTED TO LIE DOWN, BACK TO THE WIND, AND WAIT IT OUT.

ONLY BY DESPERATE URGING DID TARZAN KEEP THE FRIGHTENED CREATURE GOING.

THE WHIRLING SANDS, WHIPPED TO FURY BY THE WIND, ROLLED NEARER, BEHIND, NUMALI DREW CLOSER.

AGAIN THE PURSUER FIRED.

HOGARTH

OLD MEHARA TUMBLED TO EARTH, SCREAMING AND WHINING WITH PAIN!

NEXT WEEK: *DEATH IN THE DESERT*

Tarzan

by Edgar Rice Burroughs

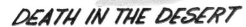

DEATH IN THE DESERT

TARZAN'S CAMEL FELL, FATALLY WOUNDED. HER AGONIZED CRIES STRUCK PITY TO THE APE-MAN'S HEART. "POOR OLD MEHARA," HE LAMENTED; "NOW YOU MAY GO TO 'THE LAST OASIS, WHERE THE GRASS GROWS SWEET AND TALL.'"

THEN SADLY HE PLUNGED HIS KNIFE INTO THE OLD FAITHFUL CREATURE TO END HER SUFFERING.

NOW NUMALI WAS DRAWING NEAR. IF TARZAN RAN, HE'D BE DROPPED BY A BULLET.

HURRIEDLY HE SCOOPED OUT A HOLE AND CRAWLED BENEATH MEHARA'S CARCASS—A TEMPORARY SHELTER AT BEST.

ANGERED BY THIS STRATEGY, NUMALI OPENED FIRE. ONE BULLET PIERCED THE CARCASS AND SCRAPED TARZAN'S ARM.

THEN THE VIOLENT SANDSTORM, SWEEPING OUT OF THE SOUTH, STRUCK WITH FULL FORCE. AS THE EERIE BROWN NIGHT ENVELOPED THE DESERT, TARZAN LEFT HIS REFUGE TO ENGAGE NUMALI HAND TO HAND.

HE CIRCLED TO CATCH THE SCENT OF HIS WILY FOE, BUT THE DRIVING SANDS CLOGGED HIS NOSTRILS.

THE SHARP PARTICLES STUNG LIKE THOUSANDS OF TORMENTING INSECTS. HE HUDDLED DOWN FOR PROTECTION.

THEN HE TOOK OFF HIS LOIN CLOTH AND USED IT AS A SCREEN TO FILTER THE ATMOSPHERE SO HE COULD BREATHE.

HOGARTH—

NEXT WEEK: TOMB OF SAND

SOON THE TORRENTS OF SAND WERE COVERING TARZAN. HAD HE ESCAPED NUMALI ONLY TO BE BURIED ALIVE?

Tarzan

by Edgar Rice Burroughs

TOMB OF SAND

IN THE RAGING WIND THE DUNES ROLLED, THREATENING TO SWALLOW TARZAN LIKE A MANY-MOUTHED MONSTER.

AT LAST THE STORM ABATED. IT WAS NIGHT—DARKENED BY THE PALL OF DUST THAT LINGERED STILL.

AGAIN TARZAN SEARCHED FOR HIS FOE—IN VAIN. HE DARED NOT RELAX FOR FEAR NUMALI WOULD FIND HIM.

WHEN DAWN CAME, NUMALI HAD VANISHED. HAD HE BEEN ENGULFED BY THE SAND, OR HAD HE ESCAPED?

TARZAN'S DEAD CAMEL, LADEN WITH PROVISIONS, WAS MISSING TOO—ENTOMBED BY THE SAND WITHOUT A TRACE.

SO WITHOUT FOOD OR WATER, TARZAN RESUMED HIS PERILOUS JOURNEY ACROSS THE TRACKLESS WASTE.

ALL DAY HE TRUDGED THE BURNING SANDS, AND ALL NIGHT, TAKING HIS COURSE FROM THE SUN AND STARS.

BUT NEXT DAY THE SKY WAS OVERCAST. NOW THERE WAS NO GUIDE IN ALL THIS CHANGELESS EXPANSE.

FINALLY HE PICKED UP A TRAIL—A TRAIL OF BLEACHED BONES, GRIM RELICS OF PERISHED CARAVANS.

—HOGARTH—

...AS THE SUN BLAZED OUT AGAIN HE BEHELD A SHIMMERING OASIS. WITH A SHOUT OF JOY HE RAN TOWARD IT. BUT HE KNEW SOON IT WAS ONLY A MIRAGE, A FANTASY OF DESERT LIGHT. THEREAFTER TARZAN'S STEP GREW SLOWER.

HIS THROAT WAS PARCHED, HIS TONGUE SWOLLEN. HIS MIGHTY STRENGTH WAS FADING UNDER THIS TERRIBLE ORDEAL!

NEXT WEEK: BLASTED HOPES

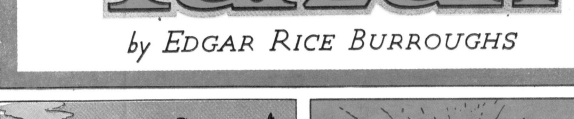

Tarzan

BLASTED HOPES

by EDGAR RICE BURROUGHS

THE MIRAGE VANISHED. TARZAN TRUDGED ON. BUT EVEN HIS IRON WILL COULD NOT LONG SUSTAIN HIS WANING STRENGTH.

HE SUCKED A PEBBLE TO ALLAY HIS BURNING THIRST. HIS BODY SEEMED AFLAME, HIS LEGS LIKE LEAD.

LATER, A VISION OF PALMS ROSE AGAIN ON THE HORIZON. TARZAN LOOKED DOWN, HE WANTED TO SEE NO MORE MIRAGES.

SUDDENLY HIS PARCHED LIPS PARTED WITH A HAPPY CRY. HERE WERE LIZARDS WHICH LIVED ONLY NEAR OASES.

TARZAN PUSHED ON WITH NEW HOPE. THE SHIMMERING VISION FOCUSED. IT WAS SOUFARA --- HIS GOAL!

AS HE DROPPED DOWN TO SIP LIGHTLY FROM A POOL, HE WAS DISCOVERED BY A MAN WHO STROLLED NEARBY.

THE MAN STARED WITH UNBELIEVING EYES, THEN HASTENED EXCITEDLY THROUGH THE GATES.

COPR. 1941, EDGAR

SOON FOUR SOUFARANS CAME TO TARZAN. "I WISH TO SEE THE EMIR," HE SAID. ONE OF THE MEN SCOWLED.

"OURS IS A FORBIDDEN CITY. THE EMIR WILL PUT YOU TO DEATH, AS IS OUR CUSTOM WITH STRANGERS."

"I WISH TO SEE THE EMIR," THE APE-MAN REPEATED. "THE RISK IS MINE." SO HE WAS LED INTO THE MAGNIFICENT CITY----

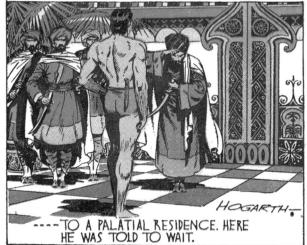

----TO A PALATIAL RESIDENCE. HERE HE WAS TOLD TO WAIT.

HOGARTH.

PRESENTLY THE DOOR OPENED. THERE STOOD, NOT THE EMIR, BUT SHEIK NUMALI, TARZAN'S MORTAL FOE!

NEXT WEEK: A LOSING FIGHT

Tarzan

by Edgar Rice Burroughs

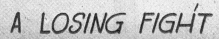

A LOSING FIGHT

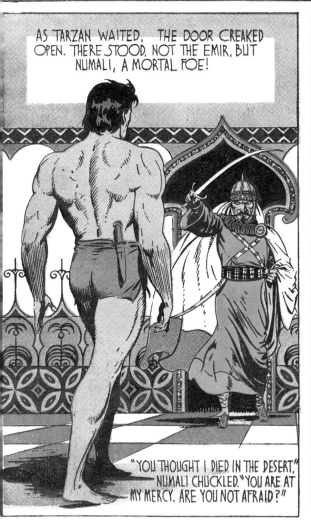

AS TARZAN WAITED, THE DOOR CREAKED OPEN. THERE STOOD, NOT THE EMIR, BUT NUMALI, A MORTAL FOE!

"YOU THOUGHT I DIED IN THE DESERT," NUMALI CHUCKLED. "YOU ARE AT MY MERCY. ARE YOU NOT AFRAID?"

"TARZAN FEARS NO MAN," THE JUNGLE LORD ANSWERED CALMLY.

THE NIMBLE APE-MAN DODGED. NUMALI VOICED A CRY OF SURPRISE AND TERROR.

ANGERED BY HIS VICTIM'S BOLDNESS, THE SHEIK DROVE HIS SWORD.

A MOMENT LATER TARZAN'S STEELY FINGERS ENCIRCLED HIS ENEMY'S THROAT.

ANSWERING THEIR MASTER'S SHOUT, FOUR MEN DASHED IN TO SEIZE THE DANGEROUS "WILD MAN."

TARZAN FOUGHT FIERCELY. NORMALLY, HE COULD HAVE ACCOUNTED FOR ALL OF THEM.

BUT HE HAD BEEN WEAKENED BY HIS DESERT ORDEAL. AT LAST HE WAS OVERWHELMED.

"HOLD HIM!" NUMALI CRIED; "I'LL RUN HIM THROUGH! THAT'S THE PROPER WAY TO MANAGE THE DOG!"

SO, TARZAN WAS HELPLESSLY PINIONED.

AND THE SINISTER SHEIK RAISED HIS SWORD TO STRIKE!

NEXT WEEK: THE TRAITOR

Tarzan

by Edgar Rice Burroughs

THE TRAITOR

AS THE HENCHMEN HELD TARZAN PINIONED, SHEIK NUMALI DROVE HIS SWORD. BUT TARZAN, SUMMONING HIS LAST OUNCE OF STRENGTH-- SWUNG ONE OF HIS CAPTORS INTO THE SWORD'S DEADLY PATH

AS NUMALI RAISED HIS SWORD ONCE MORE, A VOICE SOUNDED FROM THE DOORWAY; "HAVE YOU COME TO SUCH COWARDICE, NUMALI?"

STARTLED THE SHEIK TURNED. THERE STOOD THE EMIR IN ALL HIS MAJESTY.

"THIS MAN FOLLOWED ME FROM THE DESERT AND ATTACKED ME," NUMALI STUTTERED.

"YOU LIE," THE SOVEREIGN FROWNED. "YOUR RUFFIANS BROUGHT HIM HERE. WHO IS HE?"

TARZAN ANSWERED. "I'VE COME TO SEEK AN ALLIANCE AGAINST DAGGA RAMBA, THE BRUTAL CONQUEROR." THE EMIR SMILED: "WE'RE IN NO DANGER. THE GREAT SEA OF SAND PROTECTS US FROM INVASION."

"BESIDES, NUMALI TELLS ME DAGGA RAMBA IS ESTABLISHING PEACE AND ORDER. NOW OUR CARAVANS WILL GO UNMOLESTED."

TARZAN SHOT A SUSPICIOUS GLANCE AT NUMALI, WHO QUAILED BENEATH THAT PIERCING GAZE.

THE EMIR TOLD THE APE-MAN. "FOLLOW ME!" AS THEY LEFT, NUMALI WHISPERED TO HIS HENCHMEN:

HOGARTH—
-566-

"THEIR DAYS ARE NUMBERED. SOON MY FRIEND DAGGA RAMBA WILL COME. THEN I SHALL BE EMIR OF SOUFARA!" NEXT WEEK: SECRET VIGIL

Tarzan

by Edgar Rice Burroughs

SECRET VIGIL

AS TARZAN LEFT WITH THE EMIR, NUMALI MUTTERED: "THEY ARE DOOMED, FOR TOMORROW DAGGA RAMBA COMES!"

FASCINATED BY THE STRANGER, THE SOVEREIGN INVITED HIM TO THE PALACE. AS THEY CROSSED THE CITY, TARZAN SAW THAT THESE PEOPLE LIVED JOYOUSLY, UNDER THE ILLUSION THAT THE DESERT PROTECTED THEM FROM ALL FOES.

"TOMORROW," THE EMIR SMILED, "MY DAUGHTER TA'AMA RETURNS FROM HER VISIT TO ISTANBUL!"

TARZAN WAS PUZZLED. HE HAD LEFT TA'AMA A PRISONER OF DAGGA RAMBA. OBSERVING HIS FROWN, THE EMIR SAID:

"YOU MISUNDERSTAND DAGGA RAMBA. HE IS SURELY A KINDLY MAN. HE IS ESCORTING TA'AMA ACROSS THE DESERT."

TARZAN SAID NOTHING, BUT THAT NIGHT HE CREPT THROUGH THE SHADOWS TO WATCH NUMALI'S HOUSE

HIS SECRET VIGIL WAS SOON REWARDED. HE SAW NUMALI'S HENCHMEN COMING AND GOING WITH THE AIR OF CONSPIRATORS.

WHEN THE EMIR LEFT, TARZAN TOOK UP A POST OVERLOOKING THE DESERT, AWAITING THE OMINOUS EVENTS THAT HE WAS SURE WOULD COME!

NEXT WEEK: ULTIMATUM

NEXT DAY, DRUMS ROLLED, AND HERALDS IN THE WATCHTOWERS CRIED: "PEOPLE OF SOLFARA, REJOICE! OUR PRINCESS RETURNS!"

"CALL OUT THE GUARD OF HONOR!" THE EMIR ORDERED; "WE'LL RIDE OUT TO MEET HER. YOU, TOO, FRIEND TARZAN." THE APE-MAN SHOOK HIS HEAD. "I PREFER THAT DAGGA RAMBA BE UNAWARE OF MY PRESENCE."

HOGARTH

Tarzan

by Edgar Rice Burroughs

ULTIMATUM

AS TARZAN WATCHED, THE EMIR RODE OUT JOYOUSLY TO WELCOME TA'AMA, WHO WAS ESCORTED BY DAGGA RAMBA'S TROOP.

BUT BEFORE THEY MET, ONE OF THE DARK EMPEROR'S HORSEMEN GALLOPED OUT AND HANDED THE EMIR A MESSAGE.

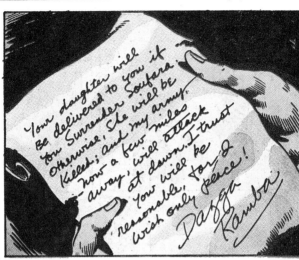

Your daughter will be delivered to you if you surrender Soufara. Otherwise, She will be killed; and my army, now a few miles away, will attack at dawn. I trust you will be reasonable, for I wish only peace! Dagga Ramba

THE EMIR GASPED; THEN TURNED SADLY BACK TO THE CITY.

THE NEWS SPREAD RAPIDLY AMONG THE PEOPLE. FEARING THE TYRANT'S MIGHT, THEY FAVORED SURRENDER.

"I WAS A FOOL NOT TO HEED YOU," THE EMIR TOLD TARZAN; "AND NOW THERE IS NAUGHT TO DO BUT SUBMIT."

"DO NOT SURRENDER UNTIL THE FINAL HOUR. MUCH MAY HAPPEN TONIGHT," TARZAN SAID MYSTERIOUSLY.

AFTER DARK, HE SLIPPED OUT TO RECONNOITRE THE CAMP OF THE ENEMY'S ADVANCE SQUADRON.

SOON HE HEARD THE DISTANT CLANK OF MARCHING MEN. "OUR MAIN ARMY ADVANCES!" CRIED DAGGA RAMBA. "I GO TO MEET IT!"

AS THE DARK EMPEROR MOUNTED HIS HORSE, HE CALLED TO HIS MEN:

"TWO OF YOU STAND GUARD INSIDE TA'AMA'S TENT. IF ANY ATTEMPT IS MADE TO TAKE HER AWAY, KILL HER—AT ONCE!"

TARZAN HAD COME TO FREE THE HOSTAGE. NOW ANY MOVE HE MADE WOULD COST HER LIFE!

HOGARTH

NEXT WEEK: FLIGHT TO DANGER

Tarzan

by Edgar Rice Burroughs

FLIGHT TO DANGER

AS DAGGA RAMBA THUNDERED AWAY TO MEET HIS MAIN ARMY, TARZAN CRAWLED TO THE ADVANCE CAMP.

IN TA'AMA'S TENT, THE GUARDS STOOD READY TO KILL HER, SHOULD ANY ATTEMPT BE MADE TO RESCUE HER.

NOW TARZAN CONCEIVED A CLEVER BUT DANGEROUS PLAN. HE CREPT UP TO TWO HORSES TETHERED NEARBY.

TO EACH HE TIED THE END OF A LONG ROPE. THEN HE SHIED THEM AWAY AT RIGHT ANGLES.

AS THEY RAN, THE ROPE STRETCHED TAUT. IT CAUGHT THE TENTS AND TOPPLED THEM. THE ASKARIS WERE SWATHED HELPLESSLY IN THE CANVAS.

ALREADY TARZAN WAS SPEEDING TO TA'AMA'S TENT. HE SLASHED THE CLOTH AND PULLED HER FREE.

THEN HE FLUNG HER ATOP A CAMEL, CLIMBED UP, AND SPURRED THE BEAST TO FLIGHT.

SOON THE ASKARIS SQUIRMED FREE. THEY OPENED FIRE, BUT THEIR TARGET WAS LOST IN DARKNESS.

TA'AMA SNUGGLED CLOSE TO TARZAN. "NOW I KNOW YOU LOVE ME," SHE PURRED WARMLY.

MEANWHILE, DAGGA RAMBA, IN A BOUNDLESS FURY, RETURNED TO THE WRECKED CAMP.

NEXT WEEK: **THE WAR SHEIK!**

"WE ATTACK THE SOUFARANS AT DAWN!" HE SHOUTED; "AND WE'LL PUT EVERY ONE TO THE SWORD!"

HOGARTH—

Tarzan

by EDGAR RICE BURROUGHS

THE WAR-SHEIK

SAFE IN HER FATHER'S PALACE, TA'AMA KISSED HER RESCUER. "YOU SHALL BE MY HUSBAND," SHE SAID.

TARZAN STOOD SILENT. "SO YOU REFUSE ME! THEN I HATE YOU!" THE GIRL CRIED, STORMING FROM THE ROOM.

"HER HOT DESERT BLOOD DOES NOT MIX WELL WITH THE BOLD MODERN WAYS SHE LEARNED IN ISTANBUL," HER FATHER SMILED.

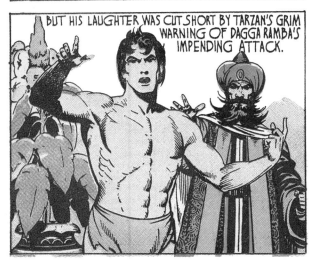

BUT HIS LAUGHTER WAS CUT SHORT BY TARZAN'S GRIM WARNING OF DAGGA RAMBA'S IMPENDING ATTACK.

"YOU SHALL BE OUR WAR-SHEIK," THE SOVEREIGN DECLARED, PRESENTING TARZAN WITH THE INSIGNIA OF COMMAND.

NOW CRIES AROSE OUTSIDE: "DOWN WITH THE EMIR! LONG LIVE NUMALI, WHO'LL GIVE US PEACE!"

"NUMALI HAS PLOTTED TO OVERTHROW ME, AND SURRENDER TO OUR FOE," THE ELDERLY RULER SAID BITTERLY.

ALREADY THE USURPER WAS RIDING UP TO TAKE OVER THE PALACE. THE EMIR CALLED TO HIS PEOPLE:

"YES—NUMALI WILL GIVE YOU PEACE, AND SLAVERY. I WILL GIVE YOU WAR, AND FREEDOM!"

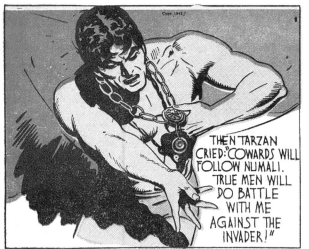

THEN TARZAN CRIED: "COWARDS WILL FOLLOW NUMALI. TRUE MEN WILL DO BATTLE WITH ME AGAINST THE INVADER!"

"LET'S HAVE DONE WITH THIS FOOLISHNESS," NUMALI SCOFFED. THEN HE GAVE A SHARP CRY OF COMMAND.

A BAND OF CONSPIRATORS, HIDDEN IN THE PALACE, SURGED OUT TO SEIZE TARZAN AND HIS ROYAL HOST! NEXT WEEK: *DANGEROUS DEFIANCE*

Tarzan
by Edgar Rice Burroughs

DANGEROUS DEFIANCE

WHEN NUMALI'S CONSPIRATORS SURGED OUT OF HIDING, THE MIGHTY APE-MAN WENT INTO ACTION.

FROM ONE HE WRENCHED A SWORD AND GAVE IT TO THE EMIR. ANOTHER HE HURLED FROM THE BALCONY.

WITH JUNGLE FURY HE FOUGHT WHILE THE CROWD ROARED IN DELIGHT.

"IF WE ARE LED BY SUCH AS HE, WE CAN VANQUISH A HUNDRED DAGGA RAMBAS."

FIGHTS BROKE OUT IN THE STREETS AMONG THE PARTISANS OF THE OLD EMIR AND NUMALI, THE USURPER.

NUMALI, SEEING HIS PLOT DOOMED, TURNED TO FLEE. TARZAN DIVED UPON HIM.

BUT BEFORE THE APE-MAN COULD CLUTCH HIM FAST, NUMALI'S HENCHMEN SPIRITED THEIR MASTER AWAY.

SO THE PLOT WAS BROKEN, AND THE PEOPLE WERE UNITED UNDER TARZAN, NEW WAR SHEIK OF SOUFARA

THE NEW DAY REVEALED DAGGA RAMBA'S ARMY IN BATTLE ARRAY ON THE DESERT READY TO ATTACK.

TARZAN WAS SURPRISED TO SEE AMONG THEM A SMALL FIELD GUN, WHICH COULD WREAK HAVOC ON THE CITY.

A COURIER RODE OUT UNDER A FLAG OF TRUCE AND SHOUTED: "OPEN THE GATES OR WE'LL BLOW THEM DOWN!"

"BLAST AWAY!" TARZAN ANSWERED DEFIANTLY.

HOGARTH—

NEXT WEEK: A FOE IN DISGUISE

571 2-15-42

Tarzan

by EDGAR RICE BURROUGHS

A FOE IN DISGUISE

WHEN TARZAN REJECTED THE ULTIMATUM, DAGGA RAMBA ORDERED HIS GUNNERS TO FIRE.

THEIR AIM WAS GOOD. THE EAST GATE WAS BLASTED, AND A CORPS OF ASKARIS CHARGED TOWARD THE BREACH.

AS THEY DREW NEAR, TARZAN SHOUTED A COMMAND. THE PATRIOTS OPENED A DEADLY FIRE.

THE ATTACKERS FELL BACK, AND DUG INTO THE SAND TO AWAIT REINFORCEMENTS.

NOW TARZAN RESOLVED UPON A DESPERATE VENTURE, AND HE CALLED FOR VOLUNTEERS.

"IT IS A DANGEROUS MISSION," HE SAID: "A SCORE OF US WILL RIDE OUT--PERHAPS NONE WILL RETURN."

ONE OF NUMALI'S HENCHMEN OVERHEARD THE DARING PLAN, AND HURRIED TO HIS MASTER'S HIDING PLACE.

"THIS IS YOUR CHANCE TO KILL TARZAN," THE SPY URGED AS HE EXPLAINED HIS PLAN.

SOON, TARZAN AND HIS BRAVE MEN RODE THROUGH THE WEST GATE. FROM A WINDOW, TA'AMA WATCHED.

"OH, TARZAN, I LOVE YOU," SHE SIGHED: "MAY ALLAH PRESERVE YOU."

SHE SAW THAT ONE WARRIOR TAGGED BEHIND THE REST. A SUDDEN GUST OF WIND BLEW BACK HIS HOOD.

HOGARTH—

TA'AMA GASPED: NUMALI! TARZAN'S FOE! HE'S UP TO SOME DREADFUL TREACHERY!"

NEXT WEEK: A VILLAIN'S STRATAGEM

Tarzan

by Edgar Rice Burroughs

WHEN TA'AMA SAW NUMALI IN DISGUISE, RIDING BEHIND TARZAN'S TROOP, SHE KNEW HE WAS UP TO DEVILTRY.

PRESENTLY SHE APPEARED AT THE ROYAL STABLES, IN RIDING GARB. "ALI! MY HORSE!" SHE CRIED

"BUT YOUR HIGHNESS CANNOT RIDE TODAY-- IT IS DANGEROUS," THE STABLEBOY PROTESTED

"MY HORSE!" THE GIRL REPEATED IMPERIOUSLY. AND SOON SHE WAS RACING THROUGH THE WESTERN GATEWAY.

ALREADY TARZAN'S TROOP WAS FAR AHEAD, BUT TA'AMA'S STEED WAS THE FASTEST IN THE REALM.

WHEN SHE DREW ABREAST OF NUMALI, WHO RODE BEHIND THE OTHERS, SHE DEMANDED: "WHY ARE YOU HERE?"

"I SHALL DEMONSTRATE," THE VILLAIN SMILED, AS HE RAISED HIS RIFLE AND AIMED AT TARZAN'S BACK.

TA'AMA JERKED HER HORSE'S REINS. THE OBEDIENT CREATURE SWERVED AGAINST NUMALI'S MOUNT.

BOTH RIDERS TUMBLED TO EARTH. IN THE FALL, NUMALI'S WEAPON WAS DISCHARGED.

THE GALLOPING HORSEMEN LOOKED BACK. TARZAN'S KEEN EYES RECOGNIZED TA'AMA AND HIS FOE.

HE WHEELED AND RACED TOWARD THEM AT TOP SPEED. BUT NUMALI QUICKLY RETRIEVED HIS MUSKET, TO PUT AN END TO THE HATED TARZAN!

NEXT WEEK: PERILOUS PURPOSE

HOGARTH— 573

Tarzan
by Edgar Rice Burroughs

AS NUMALI LEVELED HIS RIFLE AT TARZAN, TA'AMA SPRANG AT HIM. THE GUN FIRED HARMLESSLY.

NUMALI, FEARING HE COULDN'T RELOAD IN TIME, PICKED UP THE GIRL AND MOUNTED HER SPEEDY HORSE.

TOWARD DAGGA RAMBA'S CAMP HE GALLOPED, WITH TARZAN'S TROOP IN SWIFT PURSUIT.

WHEN HE REALIZED HIS HORSE WAS SLACKENED BY THE DOUBLE BURDEN, HE FLUNG TA'AMA TO THE GROUND.

AS TARZAN SCOOPED HER UP----

--HIS MEN RAISED MUSKETS TO RIDDLE NUMALI. THEN A MUSKETEER CRIED: "BULLETS ARE SCARCE. ONE IS ENOUGH FOR A TRAITOR!"

A SHOT RANG OUT. THE TREACHEROUS NUMALI PITCHED OFF INTO THE SAND----DEAD.

TA'AMA CALLED HER HORSE. AS SHE MOUNTED, TARZAN SAID STERNLY: "YOU WILL RETURN TO THE CITY."

WITHOUT A REPLY, THE GIRL TURNED HOMEWARD, WHILE THE TROOP WHEELED AND RODE AWAY.

HOGARTH—
574-

IT WAS TARZAN'S DANGEROUS PURPOSE TO CAPTURE THE SMALL FIELD GUN, WHICH WAS THE FOE'S MOST EFFECTIVE WEAPON. AS THE SQUADRON APPROACHED-----

--THE ASKARI ARTILLERYMEN SPRANG TO THE ALERT. CONFIDENTLY THEY TURNED THE GUN'S MUZZLE AGAINST THE DARING CAVALRY CHARGE!

NEXT WEEK: BESIEGED

Tarzan
by Edgar Rice Burroughs
BESIEGED

THE ENEMY ARTILLERYMEN TURNED THE GUN AGAINST TARZAN AND HIS DARING TROOP. BUT BEFORE THEY COULD FIRE, THE SOLIFARAN MARKSMEN PICKED THEM OFF.

THEN HORSES WERE HITCHED TO THE GUN, AND TARZAN'S TROOP CLATTERED BACK TO THE CITY WITH THEIR PRIZE.

TARZAN HURRIED TO THE EAST GATE, WHERE HE LAUNCHED AN ASSAULT THAT HURLED BACK THE FOE'S MAIN ARMY.

INSTEAD OF RENEWING THE FRONTAL ATTACK, DAGGA RAMBA THREW HIS FORCES AROUND THE CITY FOR A SIEGE.

DESPITE TARZAN'S ADVANCE WARNING, THE EASY-GOING SOLIFARANS HAD LAID IN NO RESERVES OF FOOD.

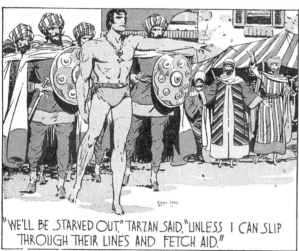

"WE'LL BE STARVED OUT," TARZAN SAID, "UNLESS I CAN SLIP THROUGH THEIR LINES AND FETCH AID."

THAT NIGHT PICKET LINES WERE TIGHTENED. EVERY FEW FEET, BRIGHT FIRES BLAZED.

"NO HUMAN BEING CAN PENETRATE THAT LINE," TARZAN MUSED; "NO HUMAN BEING---"

THEN SUDDENLY HE CONCEIVED A DESPERATE PLAN. THE RISK WAS GREAT. HE'D TAKE IT.

AN HOUR LATER, A TWO-HUMPED CAMEL GRAZED LEISURELY TOWARD THE PICKET LINE. A SENTRY WATCHED CURIOUSLY.

NEXT WEEK: THE SIGN OF DEATH

"QUEER SORT OF CAMEL," THE SENTRY GRUNTED; "THE HUMP IN FRONT SEEMS TOO LARGE.....STRANGE."

HOGARTH—

Tarzan
by Edgar Rice Burroughs

THE SENTRY APPROACHED THE CAMEL CURIOUSLY. THERE WAS SOMETHING STRANGE IN THAT FORWARD HUMP.

STRANGE IT WAS INDEED, FOR THAT FORWARD HUMP WAS TARZAN, COVERED BY A CAMEL SKIN!

THE APE-MAN PRICKED THE BEAST WITH HIS KNIFE, HOPING IT WOULD DASH THROUGH THE PICKET LINE.

THE CAMEL SQUEALED AND JUMPED. THE HIDE THAT COVERED TARZAN FLAPPED ASIDE, EXPOSING HIM.

"A MAN," THE SENTRY SHOUTED; "I KNEW THERE WAS SOMETHING WRONG." HE FIRED.

THE CAMEL FELL. TARZAN LEAPED OFF AND FLED THROUGH THE PICKET LINE INTO THE DESERT.

ASKARI PATROLS SEARCHED FOR HIM, AND THOUGH TARZAN EVADED THEM, HIS PLIGHT WAS GRAVE.

HE DARED NOT TRY TO SLIP BACK TO SOUFARA, FOR NOW HIS FOES WERE ON THE ALERT.

OVERHEAD, A VULTURE WHEELED. ITS STRANGE INSTINCT TOLD IT THAT IT SOON WOULD FEED.

SO HE DETERMINED TO TRY THE PERILOUS JOURNEY TO FETCH THE IBEK WARRIORS.

BUT ON HIS LONG DESERT TREK HIS MIGHTY STRENGTH BEGAN AT LAST TO WANE.

HOGARTH

FINALLY, THE APE-MAN FELL AND LAY STILL----FROM ITS AIRY REALM THE VULTURE GLIDED DOWNWARD!

NEXT WEEK: THE VEILED WARRIORS

Tarzan

by Edgar Rice Burroughs

TARZAN LAY MOTIONLESS ON THE DESERT SANDS. THE DEATH SCENTING VULTURE GLIDED DOWNWARD.

MEANWHILE, KAMUR DISCOVERED THAT DAGGA RAMBA'S FORTRESS WAS STRANGELY QUIET. HE ATTACKED. WHEN HIS IBEKS HAD CONQUERED THE SMALL GARRISON, HE LEARNED THAT THE MAIN ARMY HAD GONE TO SOUFARA.

KAMUR WAS ALARMED. TARZAN, TOO, HAD GONE TO SOUFARA. HE MUST BE SAVED FROM DAGGA RAMBA.

HURRIEDLY THE IBEKS BROUGHT THEIR HORSES FROM THE HIDDEN VALLEY AND ORGANIZED A RESCUE FORCE.

THEY WERE JOINED BY MANY BEDOUINS WHO HAD COME TO KNOW TARZAN AS THEIR FRIEND.

IT WAS THIS BAND THAT FOUND TARZAN AND UNDER THEIR CARE THE MIGHTY APE-MAN REVIVED QUICKLY.

"WE HAVE SAVED TARZAN," SAID ONE; "SO LET US RETURN HOME." "NO," TARZAN DECLARED; "WE GO TO FIGHT DAGGA RAMBA."

THEY SIGHTED A STRANGE TROOP. "THE FIERCE VEILED WARRIORS," ONE QUAVERED. "WE MUST ATTACK!"

BUT TARZAN WANTED PEACE WITH ALL BUT DAGGA RAMBA. DESPITE THE WARNING OF HIS FRIENDS, HE RODE OUT ALONE.

AS HE DREW NEAR TO THE STRANGERS, HE GAVE THE SIGN OF FRIENDSHIP.

—HOGARTH—

BUT INSTEAD OF RETURNING THE SIGN, THE CHIEF OF THE VEILED WARRIORS GLARED FIERCELY.

NEXT WEEK: VICTORY OR DEATH!

577

Tarzan

by EDGAR RICE BURROUGHS

VICTORY or DEATH!

"WE GO TO JOIN TARZAN, WHO IS KNOWN TO US BY HIS MIGHTY DEEDS," THE VEILED WARRIOR SAID. "ARE YOU HIS FRIEND OR FOE?"

"I AM TARZAN," THE APE-MAN SAID. THE WARRIOR DISBELIEVED HIM. HE HAD PICTURED HIS HERO AS A SUPER-GIANT.

"YOU'RE A TREACHEROUS IMPOSTOR," THE VEILED CHIEFTAIN CRIED, "AND FOR THAT YOU DIE!"

DRAWING HIS SWORD, HE SPURRED HIS CAMEL TOWARD THE JUNGLE LORD----- ----WHO REMAINED CALM AND MOTIONLESS.

BUT JUST AS THE SWORDSMAN SWUNG, TARZAN LEAPED ATOP HIS HORSE AND GRASPED THE FELLOW'S WRIST.

THEN WITH AN EASY TUG HE JERKED HIS ASSAILANT TO THE GROUND.

THE DESERT WARRIOR STRUGGLED AND FOUGHT, BUT THE POWERFUL APE-MAN HELD HIM HELPLESS UNTIL AT LAST HE SAID:

"TRUE--YOU ARE HE--THE MIGHTY TARZAN. WE SHALL BE PROUD TO SERVE UNDER YOUR BANNER."

SO WERE THE FIERCE VEILED WARRIORS ADDED TO THE FORCE THAT SPED TO LIFT THE SIEGE OF SOLIFARA ACROSS THE DESERT.

DAGGA RAMBA CAUGHT SIGHT OF THEM. HE ORDERED A QUICK ASSAULT ON THE MAIN GATE, TO GET INSIDE THE CITY.

WHEN TARZAN SAW THE ATTACK SUCCEEDING HE CALLED FOR A SWIFT, DESPERATE CHARGE.

HOGARTH

"LIGHTEN HORSES, DISCARD SUPPLIES. IF WE WIN WE'LL GET THE FOES SUPPLIES. IF WE LOSE--DEAD MEN NEED NO SUPPLIES!"

NEXT WEEK: FINAL ENCOUNTER

Tarzan

by EDGAR RICE BURROUGHS

AS TARZAN DREW NEAR, HE SAW THE INVADING HORDE STREAMING INTO SOLIFARA. AT THE END OF THE COLUMN TRAILED PACK CAMELS.

"THEY'RE LOADED WITH AMMUNITION. CUT THEM OFF!" TARZAN SHOUTED.

SOON THE APE-MAN'S LEGION WAS SLASHING LIKE A KNIFE THROUGH THE ENEMY COLUMN.

THE LADEN BEASTS OF THE AMMUNITION TRAIN WERE SCATTERED INTO THE DESERT.

SO DAGGA RAMBA'S ASKARIS WERE TRAPPED IN THE CITY, WITH NO RESERVES OF AMMUNITION.

AND NOW TARZAN LED HIS STRANGE TROOP INTO SOLIFARA TO ENGAGE THE FOE IN A LAST DECISIVE BATTLE.

THE ASKARIS, THEIR AMMUNITION SPENT, RESORTED TO BAYONETS.

BUT THESE WERE NO MATCH FOR THE SPEARS AND ARROWS OF THE WILD IBEKS.....

----AND THE ACCURATE MUSKETRY OF THE SOLIFARANS AND THEIR DESERT ALLIES.

THROUGH THE DESPERATE STRUGGLE, TARZAN DEPENDED ONLY ON HIS SWORD AND HIS STRONG RIGHT ARM.

THEN HE CAME FACE TO FACE WITH DAGGA RAMBA, WHO HAD SAVED HIS CARTRIDGES FOR THIS VERY ENCOUNTER. "SO WE MEET AGAIN," THE TYRANT SHOUTED; "BUT THIS TIME SHALL BE THE LAST!"

HOGARTH—

NEXT WEEK "CHALLENGED!"

Tarzan
by Edgar Rice Burroughs

CHALLENGED

"WE MEET AGAIN," DAGGA RAMBA SAID — "AND THIS TIME SHALL BE THE LAST." "SO SHALL IT," TARZAN ANSWERED.

CONFIDENTLY, DELIBERATELY, THE DARK EMPEROR RAISED HIS REVOLVER.

AT THAT MOMENT TARZAN HURLED HIS SWORD. THE POINT FOUND THE HEART OF DAGGA RAMBA. SO DIED THE BRUTAL TYRANT WHO HAD ASPIRED TO RULE THE DESERT AND THE MOUNTAINS.

NOW TARZAN HASTENED TO THE EMIR'S PALACE, WHICH HE FEARED WOULD BE A CENTER OF ATTACK.

HE ARRIVED IN TIME TO SEE TA'AMA BEING SPIRITED AWAY BY TWO ASKARIS. THEN— STRANGELY, HE TOSSED AWAY HIS SWORD.

"THIS IS WORK FOR A MAN'S TWO HANDS," HE GROWLED AS HE POUNCED ON THE GIRL'S CAPTORS.

HE CLAMPED THE NECK OF EACH IN THE CROOK OF AN ARM——— ———AND THROTTLED THE SCOUNDRELS

"AGAIN YOU HAVE SAVED ME. I KNOW YOU LOVE ME!" TA'AMA CRIED.

AT THAT MOMENT THE GIANT IBEK WARRIOR HETGAN STRODE INTO THE ROOM.

HOGARTH—

THOUGH HE AND TARZAN WERE ALLIES, HIS EYES BLAZED WITH SAVAGE HOSTILITY.

380   1-19-46

NEXT WEEK: DOUBLE JEOPARDY

"TAKE UP YOUR SWORD, TARZAN," THE HUGE WARRIOR ROARED; "WE FIGHT— ONE OF US MUST DIE!"

Tarzan

by Edgar Rice Burroughs

DOUBLE JEOPARDY

"WHY MUST WE FIGHT?" TARZAN ASKED WHEN HETGAN CHALLENGED HIM; "WE ARE FRIENDS." THE IBEK POINTED TO TA'AMA. "I WANT HER TO BE MY BRIDE. SINCE SHE SEEMS TO LOVE YOU, I MUST KILL YOU."

AS THE GIRL TURNED FICKLE EYES ON THE PRIMITIVE WARRIOR, A SHOUT AROSE OUTSIDE. "FIRE! FIRE!"

THE EMIR DASHED INTO THE ROOM, FOLLOWED BY A TONGUE OF FLAME. HETGAN CARRIED TA'AMA TO SAFETY——

——WHILE TARZAN SEIZED THE EMIR AND LEAPED INTO THE STREET, WHERE THE INVADERS WERE BEING MOPPED UP.

"NOW DAGGA RAMBA'S HORDE IS DESTROYED," THE APE-MAN SAID SOLEMNLY; "MY MISSION IS DONE. I GO."

SO REFUSING ALL HONORS AND REWARDS, TARZAN MOUNTED ONE OF THE CAPTURED CAMELS AND RODE AWAY.

THE DESERT CROSSED, HE PRESENTED THE BEAST TO A BEDOUIN TRIBE, THEN PASSED ON INTO THE MOUNTAINS.

ONE DAY HE WAS TRAILED BY A LION. HE COULD HAVE DISPATCHED IT EASILY, BUT HE CHOSE TO TEASE IT.

HE RAN, KEEPING JUST AHEAD, AND WHEN HE CAME TO A SCREEN OF FOLIAGE, HE LEAPED THROUGH IT.

BUT INSTEAD OF LANDING ON THE GROUND, HE FOUND HIMSELF HURTLING THROUGH SPACE, INTO A DEEP CHASM.

HIS PLUNGE WAS WITNESSED BY A STRANGE COUPLE. THE MAN SNARLED. "IF OUR VISITOR SURVIVES HIS FALL, I'LL KILL HIM." NEXT WEEK: THE STRANGE TITANS

Tarzan

by EDGAR RICE BURROUGHS

UNKNOWN TO TARZAN, THE STRANGE COUPLE WATCHED HIM HURTLE DOWN INTO THE CHASM.

AS HE STRUCK THE WATER, THE SEETHING RAPIDS CAUGHT HIM AND WHIRLED HIM DOWNSTREAM.

HIS HEAD STRUCK A ROCK. THE MIGHTY APE-MAN WAS DAZED AND WEAKENED BY THE BLOW.

"OH, I HOPE HE WON'T BE KILLED," THE GIRL SIGHED; "HE'S SO HANDSOME!"

"I MUST KILL HIM," SNARLED KALBAN MARTIUS; "IF HE LIVES YOU MIGHT FALL IN LOVE WITH HIM!"

MARTIUS RAISED THE RIFLE. OLGA SCREAMED--- AND STRUCK DOWN THE FIREARM.

A MOMENT LATER TARZAN WAS SWEPT OVER A DAM, INTO A QUIET LAKE ON THE FLOOR OF THE MYSTERIOUS VALLEY.

"NEVER MIND," MARTIUS GROWLED; "HE'LL FALL INTO THE HANDS OF THE KOLOSANS, AND THEY'LL DO AS I COMMAND."

SOON TARZAN WAS SIGHTED FROM THE VILLAGE OF THE KOLO-SANS, A STRANGE TRIBE OF GIANTS.

HE WAS JUST ABOUT TO SINK, WHEN THE TITANS TOOK HIM INTO A CANOE AND ROWED ASHORE.

THE APE-MAN LAPSED INTO UNCONSCIOUSNESS, AND THE GIANTS WERE TRYING TO REVIVE HIM, WHEN MARTIUS APPEARED. "STAND ASIDE!" THE DWARF COMMANDED. "HE MUST DIE!" *NEXT WEEK: MYSTERIOUS VALLEY*

Tarzan
by Edgar Rice Burroughs

"STAND ASIDE. THAT ONE MUST DIE!" KALBAN MARTIUS CALLED TO THE GIANTS AS HE POINTED TOWARD TARZAN. ONE OF THE KOLOSANS WHISPERED TO ANOTHER: "IF THE STRANGER IS THE DWARF'S ENEMY, THEN HE IS OUR FRIEND."

"AWAY!" MARTIUS REPEATED; "OR I'LL KILL YOU AS I HAVE KILLED ALL WHO OPPOSE MY IRON WILL!"

THE GIANTS MOVED ASIDE, FOR THEY FEARED THE THUNDERSTICK THAT SPOKE WITH DEADLY TONGUE OF FIRE.

TARZAN WAS RECOVERING FROM HIS DAZE. SUDDENLY HE SAW HIS PERIL.

THE APE-MAN SPRANG INTO THE TREE LIKE A FLASH OF LIGHTNING.

MARTIUS FIRED. BUT HE MISSED THE SWAYING FIGURE.

A MOMENT LATER TARZAN DROPPED DOWN AND DISARMED HIM. HE SHATTERED THE RIFLE AGAINST A TREE.

RELIEVED OF HIS POWER, THE TYRANT COWERED AND WHINED: "PLEASE DON'T KILL ME!"

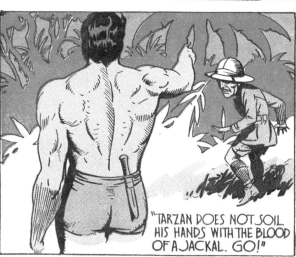

"TARZAN DOES NOT SOIL HIS HANDS WITH THE BLOOD OF A JACKAL. GO!"

AFTER THANKING THE STRANGE GIANTS FOR SAVING HIM FROM THE LAKE, THE APE-MAN STARTED AWAY. SOLEMNLY THE KOLOSAN CHIEF SAID:

HOGARTH—

"IF YOU THINK YOU CAN LEAVE THIS VALLEY, TARZAN, YOU ARE MISTAKEN." -- NEXT WEEK = JUNGLE TITAN =

Tarzan

by EDGAR RICE BURROUGHS

"YOU CANNOT LEAVE THIS VALLEY," THE KOLOSAN CHIEF REPEATED. TARZAN PAID NO HEED.

BUT SOON HE SAW WHY THIS VALLEY WAS A VAST PRISON. IT WAS ENCLOSED BY HIGH, TOWERING WALLS SMOOTH AS GLASS.

MEANWHILE, MARTIUS ENCOUNTERED OLGA. "I WAS COMING TO HELP THE HANDSOME STRANGER," SHE SAID COOLLY.

AT THAT MOMENT A MAMMOTH LION AMBLED FROM THE FOREST. KALBAN MARTIUS GRABBED THE GIRL'S RIFLE, AND FIRED.

NEARBY, TARZAN HEARD, AND RUSHED TOWARD THE SOUND. THE CARNIVORE, MADDENED BY A WOUND, WAS CHARGING.

MARTIUS THREW DOWN THE RIFLE AND FLED. OLGA PICKED IT UP, BUT TARZAN FEARED SHE COULD NOT FIRE IN TIME.

HE SPRANG ASTRIDE THE BEAST, AND CLUTCHED ITS MANE. AT LEAST HE HAD HALTED ITS CHARGE TOWARD THE GIRL.

NEVER HAD THE APE-MAN ENCOUNTERED A LION SO HUGE, BUT HE DID NOT HESITATE.

THOUGH HE FOUGHT WITH ALL HIS POWER, HE WAS NOT SURE HE COULD CONQUER THIS JUNGLE TITAN.

BUT NOW BRAVE OLGA FIRED. THE LION FELL DEAD. "OH, I'M GLAD YOU'RE NOT HURT!" SHE EXCLAIMED.

"WHO ARE YOU? WHAT IS THE MYSTERY OF THIS VALLEY?" THE PUZZLED APE-MAN ASKED.

HOGARTH—

INSTEAD OF ANSWERING, THE GIRL SHUDDERED, AND HER EYES CLOUDED WITH FEAR. NEXT WEEK.

"SURPRISE!"

Tarzan

by EDGAR RICE BURROUGHS

SURPRISE

OLGA'S EYES TURNED PLEADINGLY TO TARZAN. "I KNOW YOU WILL BE MY FRIEND. I'LL NEED YOU WHEN KALBAN---"

SHE WAS INTERRUPTED BY A GIANT GORILLA SWINGING INTO THE CLEARING. TARZAN AND THE GIRL MIGHT HAVE FLED-

---BUT IF HE HAD TO REMAIN IN THIS MYSTERIOUS VALLEY, HE MUST COMMAND THE RESPECT OF ITS CREATURES.

THE GORILLA ANSWERED CALMLY: "I BUHL-GAN. BUHL-GAN FRIEND."

THE APE-MAN BEAT HIS CHEST AND CALLED BOLDLY: "I, TARZAN, MIGHTY FIGHTER. TARZAN KILL!"

SEEING TARZAN'S SURPRISE, OLGA SMILED. "THE CREATURES HERE ARE HUGE, BUT GENTLE. ONLY KALBAN MARTIUS, THE DWARF, IS EVIL."

AS THEY SET OUT FOR OLGA'S HOME, TARZAN INQUIRED WHAT SHE WAS DOING HERE. THE GIRL ANSWERED: "MY FATHER AND MARTIUS ARE SCIENTISTS SEEKING THE SECRET ELEMENT THAT MAKES EVERYTHING GROW BIG HERE."

THE GIRL SIGHED. "FATHER BELIEVES THE SECRET CAN AID MANKIND, BUT I KNOW KALBAN WILL USE IT FOR EVIL!"

THEY HAD TRAVERSED THE JUNGLE NOW, AND TARZAN BEHELD A CASTLE, HUGE AND STRANGE. "WE LIVE THERE," SAID OLGA.

"BUT HOW DID YOU COME TO THIS VALLEY, AND HOW WILL YOU LEAVE?" TARZAN ASKED. BEFORE SHE COULD REPLY----

NEXT WEEK: **FATEFUL FOUNTAIN** —HOGARTH—

---A GIANT KOLOSAN, WHO HAD BEEN FOLLOWING, SEIZED TARZAN IN HIS MIGHTY ARMS.

Tarzan

by EDGAR RICE BURROUGHS

FATEFUL FOUNTAIN

AFTER HE HAD FLED INTO THE FOREST, THE KOLOSAN SET TARZAN DOWN AND POINTED BACK.

"YOU MUST NEVER GO NEAR THE CASTLE," HE SAID GRAVELY; "KALBAN MARTIUS DWELLS THERE. HE'LL KILL YOU."

THEN THE GIANT ADDED: "OUR ELDERS BEG YOU TO GO WITH THEM TO THE SECRET CAVERN OF THE FORBIDDEN FOUNTAIN."

SO TARZAN, EVER CURIOUS, JOINED THE SOLEMN PILGRIMAGE OF THE WISE MEN.

AS THEY PASSED THROUGH A GORGE, MARTIUS DISCOVERED THEM, AND RAN AHEAD TO HIDE.

THEN, HE CREPT UNSEEN BENEATH THE OUTSPREAD SKIN OF A MAMMOTH LION, BORNE BY CHOSEN CARRIERS.

PRESENTLY THE PROCESSION REACHED THE PORTALS OF A CAVERN, WHICH WERE SWUNG OPEN.

WITHIN THE CAVE A FOUNTAIN POURED FROM A COLOSSAL IDOL-- GOD OF EVIL POWER

A KOLOSAN WHISPERED TO TARZAN: "ONE SIP OF THOSE WATERS DOUBLES THE SIZE OF ANY LIVING THING."

COPR. 1943

THE CHIEF SPOKE: "O MIGHTY ONE RETAIN THY FORBIDDEN WATERS WITHIN THIS CAVE, THAT THEY MAY NEVER FLOW INTO OUR BELOVED VALLEY."

THE DWARF LISTENED IN AMAZEMENT. THIS WAS THE MYSTERIOUS ELEMENT OF GROWTH FOR WHICH HE HAD BEEN SEARCHING.

HIDDEN BY THE LION SKIN, HE CREPT TOWARD THE FATEFUL FOUNTAIN.

HOGARTH--

NEXT WEEK: "FROM DWARF TO GIANT"

Tarzan

by EDGAR RICE BURROUGHS   FROM DWARF TO GIANT

"WHOEVER DRINKS FROM ITS WATERS GROWS INSTANTLY HUGE AND POWERFUL," THE KOLOSAN SAID, "BUT HE LOSES HIS SOUL!"

THE EVIL HEART OF KALBAN MARTILIS WAS AFIRE. HE'D PAY ANY PRICE TO BECOME BIG AND STRONG.

HE FILLED HIS CANTEEN AND GULPED THE MAGIC WATERS. AMAZINGLY, HIS BODY MAGNIFIED.

AND NOW HE COMPLETED HIS MONSTROUS TRANSFORMATION BY THROWING THE LION SKIN ABOUT HIM.

Copr. 1943.

TARZAN LUNGED AT THE DWARF-BECOME-GIANT, BUT THE KOLOSANS SEIZED HIM, FEARING MARTILIS WOULD DESTROY HIM.

THE MONSTER CRIED OUT, "BEWARE! I AM KING OF BEASTS AND MEN!"

STILL HE FEARED THE MIGHTY APE-MAN--UNTIL HE COULD COMPLETE HIS FIENDISH PLANS. HE FLED.

SOON HE APPEARED IN THE KOLOSAN VILLAGE, HOLDING OUT THE CANTEEN, SHOUTING TO THE TRIBESMEN----

"YOUR CHIEFS HAVE DENIED YOU THE POWER YOU DESERVE. DRINK! ENTER MY WORLD OF MASTER MEN!"

LIKE ALL THINGS FORBIDDEN, THE MAGIC WATER INTRIGUED SOME OF THE KOLOSANS. ONE GRASPED THE CANTEEN.

NEXT WEEK: MONSTER MEN

MEANWHILE, TARZAN WAS TRAILING THE MONSTER, LITTLE REALIZING THE HORROR HE WAS SOON TO FACE.

HOGARTH

Tarzan

by EDGAR RICE BURROUGHS

AT MARTIUS' BIDDING, SOME OF THE KOLOSANS DRANK THE MAGIC WATER. INSTANTLY THEIR BODIES SPRANG TO DOUBLE SIZE.

A SUB-CHIEF CRIED IN HORROR. "AYE, THEY'VE BECOME HUGE AND POWERFUL, BUT THEY'RE NO LONGER HUMAN."

MARTIUS SHOUTED TO THE SUPER-GIANTS -- "IF THE OTHERS WON'T JOIN US, THEY'RE OUR FOES. KILL THEM!"

UNDER THE EVIL SPELL OF THE MAGIC WATER, THE DEMON-MEN SET UPON THEIR PEACEFUL BROTHERS.

SOME DIED, BUT MOST OF THEM FLED INTO THE FOREST.

NOW OLGA, UNAWARE OF THESE SENSATIONAL EVENTS, CAME TO THE VILLAGE SEEKING TARZAN.

TERRIFIED, SHE TURNED TO FLEE, BUT MARTIUS OVERTOOK HER IN A FEW GIANT STRIDES.

THEN TARZAN ARRIVED. "LET THE GIRL BE!" HE ROARED BOLDLY. WITH A LAUGH MARTIUS TURNED TO HIS MONSTER-MEN. "NOW TARZAN IS THE DWARF. DESTROY HIM!"

NEXT WEEK: IN GIANT HANDS

HOGARTH

SBB·6-14-42

Tarzan

by Edgar Rice Burroughs

IN GIANT HANDS

WHEN MARTIUS SET THE MONSTER-MEN UPON HIM, TARZAN SPRANG INTO A TREE.

AN INSTANT LATER HUGE HANDS THRUST UP THROUGH THE DENSE FOLIAGE AND GRASPED HIM.

AS THE GIANT HELD THE APE-MAN ALOFT, HIS COMPANIONS HOWLED WITH GLEE: "CRUSH HIM! KILL HIM!"

COOLLY TARZAN SURVEYED HIS AMAZING PLIGHT. THEN HE ACTED--WITH A TERRIFIC BLOW TO HIS CAPTOR'S JAW. THE GIANT STAGGERED AND LOST HIS GRIP. THE APE-MAN FELL FREE.

DODGING A SCORE OF CLUTCHING HANDS, HE DARTED AT KALBAN WHO HELD THE TERRIFIED OLGA.

TARZAN SPRANG UPWARD, DRIVING A STUNNING BLOW TO THE DEMON-MAN'S CHIN.

BEFORE THE GIANTS REALIZED WHAT WAS HAPPENING, THE JUNGLE LORD HAD SEIZED THE GIRL AND FLED.

THE APE-MAN WAS SOON BEYOND THE REACH OF HIS MONSTROUS FOES, BUT OLGA HAD SWOONED IN HIS ARMS.

URGENTLY HE SET ABOUT TO REVIVE HER. AT LAST SHE OPENED HER EYES. "QUICK! DO YOU KNOW HOW TO ESCAPE FROM THE VALLEY?" TARZAN ASKED. "YES--" THE GIRL ANSWERED WEAKLY.

HOGARTH

NEXT WEEK: ESCAPE CUT OFF!

BUT MARTIUS HAD FORESEEN THEIR NEXT MOVE, AND NOW HE HURRIED TO BLOCK IT.

SB9-6-21-42

Tarzan

by Edgar Rice Burroughs

BATTLE TO THE DEATH

OLGA LED TARZAN TOWARD A HUGE AIRPLANE. "THAT'S HOW WE'LL GET AWAY," SHE CRIED HAPPILY.

BUT THERE THEY FOUND MARTIUS, WHO HAD COME TO WRECK THE MACHINE AND BLOCK THEIR ESCAPE.

"THIS VALLEY WILL KNOW NO PEACE WHILE YOU LIVE," TARZAN SAID GRIMLY; "I INTEND TO DESTROY YOU!"

"GIVE ME A FAIR CHANCE," MARTIUS WHIMPERED; "I AM UNARMED. YOU HAVE YOUR KNIFE."

TARZAN THREW HIS KNIFE TO THE GROUND. "I CLAIM NO ADVANTAGE," HE SAID CALMLY.

THEN THEY CLASHED—THE MONSTROUS GIANT AND THE LITHE-MUSCLED MAN OF THE JUNGLE.

MARTIUS WAS CONFIDENT OF VICTORY BY SHEER BRUTE POWER. AND NOW OLGA, FEARING FOR TARZAN'S LIFE, PICKED UP THE KNIFE TO STRIKE MARTIUS. "GO BACK!" TARZAN SHOUTED; "I SHALL KILL HIM FAIRLY!"

THEN, IN A LIGHTNING MOVE, THE AGILE TARZAN TOSSED THE UNGAINLY CREATURE OVER A SHOULDER.

A MOMENT LATER—HIS RIGHT ARM CLAMPED HIS ADVERSARY'S THROAT IN A VISE OF DEATH.

—HOGARTH—

OLGA SHUDDERED, THEN SHE SMILED. "I'M GLAD YOU KILLED HIM. ARE WE SAFE NOW?"

AS IF IN ANSWER, WILD, FIERCE CRIES SOUNDED FROM THE JUNGLE BEHIND THEM.

NEXT WEEK—

MISFORTUNE

Tarzan

by Edgar Rice Burroughs

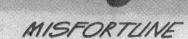

CONCEALING OLGA HIGH IN A TREE, TARZAN SPED TOWARD THE TUMULT.

IN THE JUNGLE HE FOUND THE SAVAGE GIANTS IN DEADLY COMBAT WITH THE WORTHY KOLOSANS. TARZAN SAW THAT THE TOWERING BRUTES WERE SHREWDLY DIRECTED BY THEIR CUNNING CHIEF.

SO HE HURLED HIMSELF UPON THIS EVIL GOLIATH AND SUBDUED HIM. LEADERLESS, THE SUPER-GIANTS WERE SOON ANNIHILATED.

SHAKEN BY THESE TERRIFYING EVENTS, OLGA AND HER FATHER RESOLVED TO LEAVE THIS STRANGE VALLEY.

THEIR SUPPLIES AND EQUIPMENT WERE LOADED ON THE PLANE. THEN TARZAN SUMMONED THE KOLOSANS——

"MAY NONE OF YOU EVER AGAIN DRINK THE MAGIC WATER THAT TURNS ALL LIVING CREATURES TO MONSTERS."

AS THE ENGINES ROARED, BUHL-GAN THE GORILLA CHANCED UPON MARTIUS' CANTEEN, AND DRANK THE DREGS OF THE EVIL WATER.

THE GENTLE BUHL-GAN WAS TRANSFORMED AT ONCE INTO A FRIGHTFUL BEAST.

— HOGARTH

INFURIATED BY THE NOISY MOTORS, HE CLAMBERED TO THE FUSELAGE, UNSEEN BY THE OCCUPANTS.

AS THE MACHINE STRUGGLED TO RISE, OLGA'S BROW CLOUDED "SOMETHING'S WRONG!" SHE GASPED.

591-7-5-42

NEXT WEEK: UNEQUAL COMBAT

Tarzan

by Edgar Rice Burroughs

UNEQUAL COMBAT

"SOMETHING'S WRONG WITH THE PLANE!" OLGA CRIED IN DISMAY.

BUT DESPITE HER FEARS, THE BIG MACHINE STRUGGLED INTO THE AIR AND ROSE OVER THE ESCARPMENT.

THEN THE PLANE SUDDENLY TIPPED. THE GIRL PULLED AT THE CONTROLS--IN VAIN. "WE'LL CRACK UP," SHE GASPED.

TARZAN OPENED THE DOOR TO SEE WHAT WAS WRONG. THERE, CLUTCHING A WING, WAS A GIANT GORILLA!

SOMEHOW, TARZAN DECIDED, THE BEAST MUST BE BROUGHT TO THE CENTER OF THE PLANE, TO RESTORE ITS BALANCE.

"TARZAN FIGHT! TARZAN KILL!" THE APE-MAN GROWLED.

AS HE HOPED, THE HOSTILE BEAST ACCEPTED THE CHALLENGE. "BUHL-GAN FIGHT! BUHL-GAN KILL!"

NOW THE GORILLA CRAWLED TOWARD ITS HUMAN ADVERSARY, AND THE PLANE SWAYED BACK TO AN EVEN KEEL.

BUT TARZAN REALIZED THAT BUHL-GAN MUST BE DISPOSED OF, TO ASSURE THE SAFETY OF HIS FRIENDS.

CAREFULLY BALANCING HIMSELF AGAINST THE WIND, THE APE-MAN CREPT FORWARD.

-HOGARTH-

THE IMITATIVE GORILLA DID LIKEWISE, AND THEY STOOD THERE, SQUARED FOR BATTLE-----

---TARZAN KNEW THAT SOON ONE OF THEM-PERHAPS BOTH--- WOULD BE HURTLING TO EARTH! -NEXT WEEK- EARTHWARD BOUND

Tarzan

by Edgar Rice Burroughs

EARTHWARD BOUND

WITH COOL CALCULATION THE JUNGLE LORD STRUCK THE GIANT GORILLA JUST HARD ENOUGH TO KNOCK HIM OFF BALANCE. HE HAD HOPED TO SAVE HIMSELF BY FALLING TO THE WING, BUT------

--RELIEVED OF THE BEAST'S WEIGHT, THE PLANE SHOT UP, AND TARZAN HIMSELF TOPPLED OFF!

DESPERATELY HE CLUTCHED OUT; LUCKILY HE GRASPED THE TAIL FINS.

MEANWHILE, FROM THE COCKPIT, OLGA HAD SEEN TARZAN FALL. SHE SCREAMED IN TERROR, THEN BEGAN TO SOB.

BUT A FEW MINUTES LATER, THE APE-MAN REAPPEARED, AS IF BY A MIRACLE.

WHEN SHE HAD RECOVERED FROM HER SHOCK, SHE SCOLDED: "YOU SHOULD HAVE PUT ON A PARACHUTE."

"NO TIME," TARZAN REPLIED. THEN SUDDENLY HE TENSED. AHEAD WAS ANOTHER PLANE.

HOGARTH—

"WONDER WHO IT COULD BE," THE GIRL MURMURED. "THERE'S NO AIR LINE THROUGH HERE."

NEXT WEEK: CRASH!

"THEY'RE SIGNALING US; THEY'RE IN TROUBLE," THE APE-MAN OBSERVED. (THERE'S TROUBLE AHEAD FOR YOU, TOO, TARZAN!)

Tarzan
by Edgar Rice Burroughs

CRASH!

SOMEONE IN THE CRIPPLED PLANE AHEAD WAS SIGNALING FRANTICALLY.

"THEY WANT TO TELL US SOMETHING, OVERTAKE THEM," TARZAN URGED. THEN SUDDENLY THE MYSTERY MACHINE---

---WABBLED AND FELL INTO A SCREAMING SPIN, EXPOSING THE INSIGNIA ON ITS WINGS.

"ROYAL AIR FORCE!" OLGA EXCLAIMED; "I'M AFRAID IT'S ALL OVER WITH THEM."

TARZAN SCRAMBLED BACK AND DONNED A PARACHUTE AS HE CALLED TO THE GIRL.

"YOU CAN EASILY REACH SAFETY, BUT THOSE OTHERS----THEY MAY NEED ME---IF THEY LIVE." A MOMENT LATER---

--HE WAS PLUMMETING DOWN TO EARTH. THEN THE PARACHUTE OPENED, AND LOWERED HIM THROUGH THE CLOUDS.

SOON AFTER THE PLANE CRASHED IN FLAMES ON A STRANGE ISLAND. TARZAN LANDED NEARBY AND HURRIED TO THE WRECK.

THERE HE FOUND A LONE SURVIVOR, WHO WAS ASTONISHED TO HEAR THE APE-MAN ADDRESS HIM IN ENGLISH.

HOGARTH—

"I'M WING COMMANDER JONATHAN," HE SAID; "AND I MUST REACH HEADQUARTERS. IT'S VITAL. WILL YOU HELP ME?" "THIS COUNTRY IS STRANGE TO ME," TARZAN ANSWERED, "BUT---" AT THAT INSTANT A VOICE BOOMED OUT.

"IT'S NOT LIKELY EITHER OF YOU WILL LEAVE THIS ISLAND ALIVE."

=NEXT WEEK= MAN HUNT!

Tarzan

by Edgar Rice Burroughs

MAN-HUNT—

TARZAN AND HIS COMPANION TURNED TO FACE THE THREATENING STRANGER. "WHY DO YOU WISH TO KILL US?" TARZAN ASKED COOLLY. "WE HAVE DONE NO HARM."

"I AM NAHRO THE HERMIT," THE STRANGER GROWLED; "I HATE ALL MEN. I CAME TO THIS ISLE TO BE FREE OF THEM!"

"BUT SURELY YOU WOULD NOT KILL US IN COLD BLOOD," WING COMMANDER JONATHAN PROTESTED.

"NO—THAT WOULD BE NO FUN. I'M A HUNTER. I'LL HUNT YOU DOWN LIKE WILD BEASTS."

AS THE HUNTER BACKED AWAY, HE WARNED: "I'LL GIVE YOU TILL DAWN TOMORROW TO PREPARE. THEN THE HUNT BEGINS."

"THE MAN'S CRAZY," SAID JONATHAN. "IT WILL BE EASY FOR US TO CROSS THE RIVER AND ESCAPE."

BUT FROM THE MUDDY SHORE THEY SAW THEY WERE TRAPPED. THE RIVER SWARMED WITH CROCODILES.

AS DUSK FELL, THE APE-MAN BUILT A REFUGE IN THE TREES FOR THE INJURED AVIATOR.

THAT NIGHT TARZAN SLEPT CALMLY. AT DAWN HE SPRANG AWAKE, TENSE AND ALERT. THE ZERO HOUR HAD COME.

LEAVING THE FLIER IN THE TREES, HE ROAMED THE ISLAND— —HUNTING THE HUNTER.

BUT HE FOUND NEITHER THE HERMIT NOR HIS HABITATION. HOW COULD HE HAVE VANISHED FROM THE MYSTERIOUS ISLE? —NEXT WEEK: "BETWEEN TWO FOES"

—HOGARTH—

Tarzan

by Edgar Rice Burroughs

BETWEEN TWO FOES

TARZAN TRIED TO SHAPE A BOW—IN VAIN THE MOIST WOOD LACKED SPRINGINESS.

SO HE HAD NOTHING BUT HIS KNIFE AS A WEAPON AGAINST HIS FOE'S LONG-RANGE RIFLE. SO HE SET OUT AGAIN—————

TO SEARCH FOR THE DANGEROUS HERMIT—TO KILL FIRST OR BE KILLED!

BUT SLY NAHRO KEPT TO HIS HIDING PLACE, HOPING TO UNNERVE TARZAN BY THE MYSTERY OF HIS DISAPPEARANCE.

AT MIDDAY THE APE-MAN WAS EXPLORING A SECTION OF SWAMPLAND, WEIRD AND DISMAL.

AS HE PENETRATED THE SWAMP ALONG A PENINSULA OF DRY LAND, HE TURNED SUDDENLY AS WAS HIS EVER CAUTIOUS HABIT.

THERE, IN THE DISTANCE HE SAW THE HUNTER, WHO HAD MYSTERIOUSLY REAPPEARED TO STALK HIM.

AS TARZAN HURRIED TO LOSE HIMSELF IN THE SWAMP, HE SAW A HUGE RHINOCEROS.

THE EYES OF THE RHINO WERE WEAK, BUT THE WIND BORE TO ITS KEEN NOSTRILS THE HATED SCENT OF THE INTRUDER.

THE FEROCIOUS BEAST PAWED THE EARTH, SNORTING WITH FURY.

TARZAN MIGHT HAVE ESCAPED, BUT NOW HE CONCEIVED A PLAN THAT REQUIRED HIM TO KILL THE MIGHTY MONSTER. BOLDLY HE STRODE FORWARD. THEN THE RHINO CHARGED! —NEXT WEEK— PIT OF DEATH!

Tarzan
by Edgar Rice Burroughs

THE FIERCE RHINOCEROS CHARGED STRAIGHT AT TARZAN.

FROM AFAR, NAHRO SAW THE DEADLY RUSH, AND HE WAS ANGRY THAT THE BEAST WOULD ROB HIM OF HIS PREY. HE SAW NO MORE.

NOW THE AGILE APE-MAN SPRANG OVER HIS JUNGLE ADVERSARY.

THEN HE WHIRLED, AND AS THE RHINO WAS CARRIED FORWARD BY ITS MOMENTUM, HE LEAPED ASTRIDE IT.

AGAIN AND AGAIN HIS SHARP KNIFE PIERCED THE THICK HIDE. EACH THRUST QUICKENED THE BEAST'S FURY.

AS THE JUNGLE LORD EXPECTED, THE RHINO LAY DOWN AND ROLLED OVER TO DISLODGE ITS TORMENTOR.

THEN TARZAN, WHO KNEW THE PRECISE ANATOMY OF EVERY BEAST, STRUCK AT ITS HEART. SOON THE RHINO WAS DEAD.

NOW, ACCORDING TO HIS PLAN, TARZAN CUT OFF THE FEET OF HIS VICTIM, AND DRAGGED THE CARCASS INTO A DEEP POOL.

THEN, FASTENING THE FEET OF THE RHINO TO HIS OWN HANDS AND FEET, HE STRODE INTO THE SWAMP ON ALL FOURS.

WHEN NAHRO ARRIVED HE SAW THE FOOTPRINTS, AND JUDGED THE RHINO HAD KILLED TARZAN AND STAMPED HIM INTO THE MUD.

MEANWHILE, THE APE-MAN FAR OUT IN THE SWAMP, STEPPED INTO A PIT OF QUICKSAND.

HOGARTH—

NEXT WEEK— IN A TRAP

LIKE A DEVOURING MONSTER, THE SHIFTING SANDS BEGAN TO SWALLOW HIM. THE HARDER HE STRUGGLED, THE DEEPER HE SANK.

Tarzan
by Edgar Rice Burroughs

IN A TRAP

TO SAVE HIMSELF FROM THE QUICKSAND, TARZAN TRIED TO REACH A VINE THAT HUNG FROM A DEAD TREE.

BUT THE HARDER HE STRUGGLED, THE DEEPER HE SANK.. INTO THE DEVOURING PIT.

NOW HE SAW A LITTLE MONKEY IN THE TREE, GAZING AT HIM INDIFFERENTLY. "SWING TO ME!" THE APE-MAN CALLED. AT FIRST THE MONKEY WAS STARTLED THAT A MAN-THING COULD SPEAK THE JUNGLE TONGUE.

THEN IT OBEYED. THE APE-MAN GRASPED THE VINE AND CLAMBERED INTO THE TREE.

MEANWHILE NAHRO WAS STUDYING THE FOOT-PRINTS OF THE RHINO WHICH HE THOUGHT HAD KILLED TARZAN.

SUDDENLY HE FROWNED. THERE WAS SOMETHING WRONG. A HEAVY RHINO WOULD HAVE MADE DEEPER FOOT-PRINTS.

"SOME TRICK OF TARZAN'S," HE GROWLED AS HE SET OUT TO FOLLOW HIM.

TARZAN SAW HIS FOE APPROACHING. HE SAT QUIETLY, HOPING NAHRO WOULD STEP INTO THE QUICKSAND. BUT THE HERMIT KNEW THE REGION WELL

HE WALKED AROUND THE PIT OF DEATH. WHEN THE MONKEY SAW NAHRO, IT SCREAMED, FOR IT FEARED THE EVIL HUNTER. THEN NAHRO LOOKED UP AND SAW TARZAN.

IN THE TREE THE APE-MAN MADE A PERFECT TARGET—-AND THERE WAS NO MEANS OF ESCAPE.

NEXT WEEK-MAROONED

HOGARTH

Tarzan

by Edgar Rice Burroughs

MAROONED

"YOU THOUGHT TO TRICK ME," NAHRO CHUCKLED; "BUT I AM TOO SMART FOR YOU!" FOR A MOMENT, TARZAN BELIEVED THE END HAD COME, FOR ESCAPE APPEARED IMPOSSIBLE.

THEN AN IDEA FLASHED INTO HIS MIND. HE SEIZED THE VINE BY WHICH HE HAD ASCENDED TO THE BRANCH.

THE END OF THE VINE SNAPPED LIKE A WHIP-LASH AGAINST NAHRO'S HANDS. HE DROPPED THE RIFLE.

HE FLIPPED IT, AND THE IMPULSE TRAVELED DOWN IT LIKE A RACING SERPENT.

AS HE CLUTCHED FRANTICALLY TO RETRIEVE IT, THE EVIL HERMIT FELL INTO THE PIT OF DEATH.

AND WHILE TARZAN AND THE LITTLE MONKEY WATCHED CALMLY, NAHRO WAS SWALLOWED UP BY THE QUICKSAND.

NOW THE APE-MAN RETURNED TO THE INJURED AVIATOR AND REMOVED HIM FROM THE REFUGE IN THE TREES.

"OUR ENEMY IS DESTROYED," THE APE-MAN SAID SOLEMNLY.

"NOW WE MAY FIND A WAY TO LEAVE THIS CURSED ISLAND," THE FLIER CRIED EAGERLY.

TARZAN FROWNED AS HE WATCHED THE RIVER TEEMING WITH CROCODILES. THERE SEEMED TO BE NO WAY TO SURMOUNT THOSE WATERS OF CERTAIN DEATH.

NEXT WEEK— INVITATION TO DISASTER!

HOGARTH

Tarzan

by EDGAR RICE BURROUGHS

TARZAN FROWNED. HOW COULD HE TRANSPORT THE INJURED AVIATOR ACROSS THE CROCODILE-INFESTED STREAM?

SOON THEY CAME TO ANOTHER PART OF THE ISLAND WHERE THE GAP WAS SHORTER, BUT STILL THERE WAS NO WAY TO CROSS. BUT THE OPPOSITE BANK WAS FILLED WITH VINE-STRUNG TREES, AND A TRIBE OF APES WANDERED THERE.

TARZAN CALLED: "SWING TO ME ON THE VINES!" THE APES WERE ASTONISHED AT THE MAN-THING WHO SPOKE THEIR TONGUE.

THEN, IGNORING THE STRANGER, THE FICKLE CREATURES RETURNED TO THEIR OWN AFFAIRS. SO TARZAN THREW STONES AND THE BEASTS WERE ENRAGED. "WE KILL MAN-THING!" SHOUTED BONG-TOH, THEIR KING.

AND SOON THEY WERE SWINGING ACROSS THE RIVER ON VINES.

THEY LANDED IN THE TREES OPPO-SITE, BUT THEY DID NOT THINK TO SECURE THE VINES FOR THEIR RETURN.

BUT ONE VINE CAUGHT IN A TREE AS TARZAN HOPED THIS MIGHT BRIDGE THE GAP FOR HIM AND JONATHAN.

NOW, HOWEVER, THE APES WERE SWARMING TO THE GROUND WITH THE HIDEOUS KILL-CRY ON THEIR LIPS. "YOU MUST HIDE," TARZAN URGED JONATHAN. "YOU, TOO," THE AVIATOR SAID; "YOU WILL BE KILLED." "PERHAPS," TARZAN SHRUGGED, "BUT THERE IS JUST ONE CHANCE————"

600-9-6-42   —HOGARTH—   =NEXT WEEK= BATTLE CLASH